Paulina,

Anything

When you

Big!!

Luis Vazquez-Bello

Pauline,

Anything is possible
When you dream
a...

L. vazquez Bello

THE
REALM

LUIS VAZQUEZ-BELLO

abbott press

Abbott Press books may be ordered through booksellers or by contacting:

Abbott Press
1663 Liberty Drive
Bloomington, IN 47403
www.abbottpress.com
Phone: 1 (866) 697-5310

ISBN: 978-1-4582-1943-5 (sc)
ISBN: 978-1-4582-1944-2 (hc)
ISBN: 978-1-4582-1945-9 (e)

Library of Congress Control Number: 2015915910

Print information available on the last page.

Abbott Press rev. date: 11/11/2015

CHAPTER 1

The Storm

"Wait, so is the story real? Did that really happen?" Michael asked.

"Let's start from the beginning," his father responded.

It was one of those rare stormy nights. The wind was howling as a vicious storm came through the Town of Vance Bridge. The lightning lit up the sky while thunder shook every house in the town. That's where we first meet Ryan Shepard, an eighteen-year-old who just finished his senior year of high school. Throughout his high school years, Ryan was your typical teenager who loved to party, flirt with girls, and have fun. He was an amazing athlete; at six-four, he was the star center fielder on the school's baseball team, and he was all set to attend a local university on a full athletic scholarship. That was until the day he lost his best friend—and his way.

It was only a few weeks until graduation, and Ryan was working out on the baseball field, taking in fly balls, when his coach called out to him and asked him to come inside. The coach's voice was stoic and serious. The clang of Ryan's cleats hitting the pavement leading to his coach's office seemed to resonate louder with each step he took. As he reached the door of the office, he was asked to take a seat and shut the door. "Ryan, I am so sorry to tell you this, but your father was in an accident. He passed away."

1

Two months later, Ryan was in his room on the second floor of his two-story house as the storm howled, his television tuned to a local news channel. The screen was flashing "Breaking news: Communist dictator Fernand Cartal dead at 58." The newscaster spoke of the horrors that Fernand Cartal committed as the leader of a South American country, murdering and destroying the lives of thousands during his twenty-five-year reign. His room was a mess, his clothes and books strewn all over the floor. Next to a plate of food on his desk was the business card of a Dr. Cameron Ronaldo, a local psychologist. And there lying sound asleep in bed was Ryan, until lightning struck near the house and the accompanying thunder shook the room. Ryan sat up in his bed and looked around. Noticing the television was still on, he began to get up to turn it off when suddenly another round of lightning and thunder caused the house to tremble. Ryan went and took a look out the window to see the storm. As he stared out, he saw the trees swaying ferociously. The power of the wind tossed tiles from nearby houses across the street. More lightning struck, followed by more thunder—all went dark.

Light entered Ryan's eyes. He felt water dripping onto his face, as he was staring at the ceiling of his room. The window in his room had shattered. Rain and wind were flying in. With a throbbing pain on his head, Ryan placed his right hand on his forehead. His hand came back red. Ryan sat up. The blood was thick on his hand and dripping down his face, saturating his shirt. As he moved his arm up to grab the desk next to him, he knocked over a picture frame. As soon as he had found his balance, he became dizzy and wobbled back to the ground. His hand hit the fallen frame. He picked it up and stared. It was a picture of him and his dad, Clarion Shepard, at a baseball game, with Ryan showing off a baseball in his right hand.

Ryan began to think of that day. He was fourteen years old, and he and his dad had spent three hours sitting in the stands, cheering and yelling for their favorite team for nine straight innings. They ate their favorite Italian sausage sandwich, French fries, and soda. In the seventh inning, the star player hit a foul ball while his dad ate his sandwich. As the ball descended down, Ryan's dad put up his right hand, his drink was in his left hand and his sandwich in his mouth. He caught the ball, sending the crowd into a frenzy. They laughed about it for the rest of night, and when the last pitch was thrown, Ryan's dad whispered, "There is no one I would rather go to a game with than you, son."

As Ryan gazed at the picture, he noticed a tree branch near where the picture had fallen. With glass shattered on the ground and a throbbing pain in his head, Ryan realized the branch must have knocked him out. Finally able to pull himself up from the ground, Ryan placed the frame back on the desk, and as he did, he heard three loud knocks coming from downstairs. Thinking it was from the storm, Ryan ignored it, changed out of his blood soaked shirt and lay back down in his bed. As he lay looking up at the ceiling, the wind continuing to howl outside, he heard a new round of knocks, louder than before. This time, Ryan began to feel nervous. He stood up and headed to the door of his room. Hoping his mother had been awakened by the sound, he called out to her from across the hall. She did not respond. When he reached the bedroom door, lightning illuminated the room, and there was another loud thump. He realized that the noise was coming from the front door downstairs.

Ryan felt as if he was moving in slow motion, as lightning lit up the house and thunder shook the floor. Ryan passed his mother's room as he walked down the hallway. When he reached the top of the stairs, he looked down, afraid of what was behind the door. The wood floors creaked as he walked down the stairs, holding on to the railing with his left hand. He made his way to the door. Before he opened it, he gazed out the window next to it—he saw no one. He reached out for the door handle and slowly twisted the knob. As the door swung open, he popped his head outside and saw nothing. With the wind and rain still coming down, he walked outside to the front porch. "Who is there?" he screamed out as the rain fell onto his clothing. No response. Ryan went back into the house and closed the door. He quickly locked it and was walking back toward the stairs when the knocking came again.

Ryan turned around, went to the front of the door, and looked through the peephole. He saw no one. He grabbed the knob and opened the door, and before he could shout out, he noticed it was silent. No rain. No wind. No thunder. All he heard was a clanging noise coming from below him. He looked down and saw a string on the handle with a dangling key.

The key was about seven inches long and made of shiny gold. Ryan held the key in his hand and rubbed it with his fingers. As he did, a word appeared on the side: *CREDERE*. Not knowing what the word meant or what to do with the key, Ryan placed it in the right pocket of his jeans and closed the door. In a daze, Ryan walked back up the stairs and into his bedroom. He entered the room and lay down on his bed, unsure of what to make of the key that was in his pocket.

While lying on the bed, Ryan thought of the last conversation he had had with his father. "When were you going to share this with me?" his dad yelled out as he slammed down a piece of paper on the dinner table in front of Ryan. It was his most recent report card from school, showing a 2.5 grade point average.

"It's not a big deal, Dad. I had one bad quarter, and I have a lot going on with baseball."

Ryan's comments infuriated his father, who began to tell Ryan how sports should always come second to schoolwork. "One day your baseball career will be over, and you will need something to fall back on."

Ryan blew off the comments and told his dad school wasn't his first priority anymore, grabbed his school bag, and left the house, slamming the door on his way out. That was the last time he saw or spoke with his father.

Ryan stared at the ceiling, as the lights in the house began to flicker. The streetlights outside were flickering as well—until all went dark. It was pitch-black in the house and outside. Ryan rummaged around for his cell phone, which was somewhere on the floor. Finding it, he pressed a button, and the phone lit up the room. He got up and shined the light in front of him. Out of the corner of his eye, he could see a white light through the broken window in his room. Ryan walked toward the window to look out. He saw a light flashing from the forest several blocks from his house. As he stared out, the light became brighter and eventually lit up the neighborhood. Just as quickly, it vanished, leaving only darkness again. Confused by the events of the night, Ryan began to turn around when the light reappeared in the distance. Determined to figure out where the light was coming from, Ryan put on a pair of shoes and swiftly walked downstairs in the dark, the light of his cell phone guiding him. He opened the front door, stepped outside into the quiet, black night, and made his way toward the light.

By the light of the moon and his cell phone, Ryan walked down the lonely street. There was much debris along the street. In one instance, a large tree had nearly destroyed a neighbor's car; however, a fence had broken its fall. Next to the car was a fallen basketball hoop. Staring at it, Ryan remembered the times that his dad would play outside with him for hours. Ryan and his dad, both so competitive, would play HORSE or one-on-one, neither wanting to give the other an inch. Ryan's mom would always have to yell out for them to come inside for dinner, but they would keep going. He wanted to win so badly, but being out there with his father made him so happy. Eventually, Ryan became bigger, stronger, and faster, so the games would go his way, but his father challenged him nonetheless, as he enjoyed their quality time just as much as his son did.

Continuing down the street, Ryan found it odd no one else was outside sifting through the debris and damage from the storm. Each house he passed was completely in the dark. As he looked forward, the light ahead was no longer flashing but radiating through the night. Passing the final few houses before reaching the forest, excitement and nervousness took ahold of Ryan as he wondered where the light could be coming from.

CHAPTER 2

To the Light

The deafening silence accompanied him as Ryan stared out at the forest in front of him. Using the light ahead to guide him, Ryan made his way into the forest. There were no animals scurrying along and no movement among the trees. Each step he took, each twig he stepped on, and each branch he pushed aside brought him closer, and even as he approached the light, the brightness never affected his vision or forced him to turn away—the light was captivating. Finally nearing his destination, Ryan heard a lurid growl. He looked around but saw nothing. Afraid of being attacked, he decided it was time to turn back and go home.

At that moment, Ryan felt a terror he had not felt since the day his father passed. After the conversation with his coach, he left the school in disbelief. His tears flowing uncontrollably Ryan jumped into the driver's seat of his white Ford Explorer and drove as fast as he could—disregarding the speed limits. Ryan prayed throughout the entire drive to the hospital. He said every prayer he knew, hoping for a miracle, desperate for another chance to talk with his father. He promised anyone listening to his prayers that he would give up everything for his father to be okay. Once he arrived, he parked his car and darted to the front entrance of the hospital. Quickly learning what floor his father was on, he ran down the hall and onto an elevator. He could feel his heartbeat thumping in his ears. His palms were sweaty and his fingers slipped as he tried to push the button to the fifth floor. As the elevator door slowly opened, reality was thrust into his face, as the first person he saw was his mom, weeping. Ryan stepped out of the elevator and he locked his eyes with his mother, her face said it all. As he walked toward her, he began to feel light-headed. His legs became weak and wobbled, and before he could reach his mom, he crashed down to the floor. As Ryan's body hit the cold, hard ground, his cell phone dropped out of his pocket, and as his vision began to fade, he noticed his phone displayed one missed call and a voicemail from his father.

Back in the forest, Ryan turned to head back home, and as he moved the light in the forest disappeared. No longer able to see in front of him, Ryan saw two yellow, beady eyes glowing in the distance and heard another growl. Knowing it was time to run, Ryan frantically moved as fast as he could. As he ran, he could hear the animal right behind him. He moved forward until he tripped over a root from a nearby tree and crashed into the ground. Lying face down in the dirt, he could feel the breath of the animal on his neck. He waited for the creature to devour him, yet nothing happened. He found the courage to lift up his head and face the creature but when he looked up he did not see the animal he feared; instead he saw a wooden shed.

Why was this shed in the middle of the forest? He lifted himself off the ground. Walking toward the shed, Ryan noticed that the front door had the words "*Sequere Me*" inscribed into the wood. He uttered the words, and a light appeared from inside the pocket of his jeans. Bewildered, he stuck his hand in the pocket and pulled out the Key. The word on the Key—*Credere*—was glowing. He brushed the word on the key with his fingers, and immediately the light he had been following reappeared in front of him, permeating from two small windows in the front of the shed and seeping from the bottom of the front door. Ryan, once again able to see in the shadows of the night, crept closer to the shed.

As he neared the door, he noticed symbols and drawings which were foreign to Ryan, carved into it. Continuing forward, he saw that the light from the Key had become brighter. He spotted a circular keyhole in the door and, without hesitation, placed the Key inside. It was a perfect fit. With curiosity brimming through his entire body, he turned the Key. The door swung open as a gust of wind blew from the inside, as if the door had been sealed for years. As the door swung wide-open, the light from inside quickly evaporated—leaving only darkness. Reaching for his cell phone, Ryan lit up the room with its light. He moved the phone light around to see inside the shed. No bigger than his bedroom, the shed was furnished with four tables located in the four corners of the room. He walked towards the table in the far right hand corner, using the light of the phone as his guide. There were hundreds of black and white pictures of men and women of all ages scattered on the table. He picked up several of the photos and began to analyze them—based on the clothing, the pictures seemed to range from hundreds of years ago to present-day. While the people varied in age and gender, one thing remained the same—they each stood at the front of a similar boat. He placed the photos back and continued to look around. Ryan noticed a rug in the center of the room. The rug had a thick white outline and blue in the middle. The word *Contego* was inscribed in the rug.

Ryan bent down and shone the light from the phone onto the rug. As he gazed at it, he whispered, "*Contego.*" Seconds later, a light burst from under the rug, filling the entire room. Ryan straightened out and looked around the now-lit room. He gazed at the symbols, drawings, and words on the walls. What captured his attention most were four words, one on each of the four walls: *Benevolentia, Bonitas, Misericordia,* and *Amor.* After reading each of the words, Ryan's eyes went back to the rug and the light coming from under it. He grabbed the right corner of the rug, lifted it, and pulled it to the side. Beneath the rug was a small, wooden square door with a metal handle. Seeing the light peeking out from the edges of the door, Ryan succumbed to his curiosity, grabbed the handle of the door, and lifted it up. Once again, Ryan felt a gust of wind. He poked his head through and looked down. He saw metal steps attached to the wall leading straight down with no end in sight. Since he had come this far, Ryan thought he might as well take a chance. He got down on his stomach and put his right foot on the first rail and began to climb down.

CHAPTER 3

To the Unknown

Holding onto the rails, he made his way down the metal staircase. The feeling of uneasiness in his stomach brought him back to when Ryan was fourteen and his friends convinced him to spray-paint his elementary school at night. With an apprehensive feeling in the pit of his stomach, Ryan climbed the fence of the school with his friends. They whispered and laughed as they thought of the faces of their teachers the next day. As they got closer to the school, Ryan began to sweat. He was usually a reserved kid who never got into any type of trouble. As they began to spray-paint, a security guard in the distance shouted, "Hey! What are you kids doing?" The four of them raced toward the fence, when a second security guard grabbed Ryan and held him down. The first thought in Ryan's head was how mad and ashamed his parents would be, especially his father. The security guards did not notify the police, but worse they called each of their parents. Sitting and waiting for his parents to arrive was one of the most agonizing moments in Ryan's life. When his parents got there, his dad stepped out of the car looking disappointed. "Let this be the last time," his dad said as he sat next to Ryan. His father lectured Ryan and grounded him for a month, but what stood out to Ryan about that night were the following words: "Remember, son—in life, all you have is your name. When you lose that, you lose yourself."

Ryan reflected on that moment as he continued his journey down. The light from below had illuminated his way until it began to flicker. Ryan began to regret his decision and desperately wished he was back in his room. He grabbed the rail above him and stretched out his arm to climb upward when the light abruptly vanished and all went dark. He could see nothing above or below him. He attempted to take a step up, but his left foot missed the step. As he attempted to regain his balance, he slipped again and fell down the passage.

Ryan felt an excruciating pain in his back and opened his eyes to darkness. Unable to see anything, Ryan reached into his pocket, grabbed his phone, and lit up his surroundings. Still on his back, he lifted the phone up in the air and saw the passage he had fallen from. Ryan gathered himself and eventually pushed himself off the ground to sit up when he heard a voice whisper his name. As he winced in pain he moved his phone in all directions—he saw no one.

"Who's there?" he shouted.

No one responded. As he moved the light, he noticed he was in a cave. He stood up and walked forward gingerly, and as he did, his pocket lit up once again. He pulled out the Key, as *Credere* was glowing. He put it back in his pocket, and the light dwindled away. Continuing his trek forward, he heard a splash near his feet. Directing the light of the phone toward the ground, he noticed he was standing in a shallow pool of water. He gazed forward and saw what looked like a lake. There was nowhere for him to go. Ryan took a step back out of the water and pondered his next move. As he did, a rumbling noise surrounded him and the cave shook. The earthquake-like movement lasted for five seconds and then stopped. "Ryan," the voice whispered. Ryan shouted out, but again, no one responded. He looked around and saw in the distance a light coming from above the water and moving toward him.

CHAPTER 4

Three of a Kind

The light crept closer to where Ryan stood. He observed it and noticed it had the same white glow as the one he had seen from his house and in the forest. As the light approached, the large pool of water came into better view. The water was crystal clear and went further than his eyes could see. He looked all around and saw he was in a circular cave built around thousands of boulders. Ryan saw a small sailboat in the distant waters—in the boat were three young passengers and a dog. As the boat moved closer, Ryan noticed that the three boys appeared to be triplets, as they looked similar in age, facial features, height, and build. One of the three boys was standing at the front of the boat and holding a small lantern, which was the source of the light. The dog next to the boy was a mix between a beagle and a basset hound.

"Is that really him?" said the boy steering the boat.

"Thought he would be older," said the boy sitting in the back. "He is the one who is supposed to save us?"

The first of the passengers to greet Ryan was the dog, who came to Ryan wagging his tail. Utterly confused by where the boys had come from, Ryan bent down and pet the friendly dog, who jumped up and knocked him down. Ryan rubbed its slobbery face until one of the boys shouted out, "Come Nigel." The dog quickly went to the boy's side.

As Ryan stood up, one of the boys walked toward him and said, "We don't have much time to waste. We have already waited for you long enough."

Thinking this was a joke, Ryan offered a halfhearted smile.

"My name is Rodney," the boy continued, "and this is Derrick and Andy."

Ryan gestured a hello quickly to each of them, but before he could speak, the whispering voice repeated his name. Quickly turning around to find the source of the whisper, he noticed something moving along the cave walls above him—snake-like creatures.

"Did you hear that noise?" Ryan asked.

The boys stared at him, blankly.

"How about those creatures moving through the walls?" he asked.

Now the faces of the boys revealed concern. "I think we have to go," said Andy.

Ryan asked the boys what was going on. The three boys sighed in unison. "How can he be the one to save us?" Derrick cried, incredulous.

"I'm going to what?!"

The three boys got behind Ryan and pushed him toward the boat. Nigel, who was at the front of the boat, began to howl in the direction of the cave walls to their left. As he howled, the cave began to tremble. With Ryan finally on the boat, the boys pushed off the shore as Andy grabbed the lantern and turned up the light. As the cave rattled all around the boat, they sailed off into the endless water ahead.

"Where are we going? And where am I?" Ryan shouted as the boat moved slowly and steadily.

The three boys looked at one another and whispered amongst themselves. Rodney then turned, faced Ryan, and asked, "Do you have the Key?"

Ryan placed his hand over his pocket. "Yes."

"All we can say is that we are here to pick you up. He will tell you the rest," said Andy, straight-faced.

Frustrated by their vagueness, Ryan asked who "he" was, but the three boys turned around at the same time, facing away from Ryan.

Giving up, Ryan sat down and stared into the distance as Nigel, the only one paying attention to him, came over and sat beside him. He gazed at the water behind him as he pet Nigel; the light from the lantern providing visibility. As he stared at the water, someone appeared to be floating below the surface. The image was of a man whose body and flesh seemed to have been ravaged by an animal. Ryan closed his eyes and counted to ten, and when he looked back, the body was no longer there. Attributing the disturbing vision to exhaustion, Ryan said nothing to the boys, closed his eyes, and fell asleep.

"Okay, so what do you do when a girl walks into the room and you are sitting down?" Ryan's father asked his son as he showed him how to make a tie.

"Come on, Dad, give me a hard one. I stand up when she walks in."

His father folded the tie for his son and continued discussing different scenarios that could arise at Ryan's first high school dance.

"Dad, is it normal for me to be so tense and nervous about tonight?" Ryan asked.

"Son," his father replied, "that just means you're alive."

Ryan opened his eyes, letting light in as he woke up on the boat.

"They are close to getting through, and we are running out of time. We knew this day could come; it's what we signed up for," Ryan heard a voice whisper.

Nigel, noticing Ryan was awake, went over and began to lick his face. The boys noted as well and discontinued their discussion. Rodney, holding the lantern, raised the brightness of the light. Staring at the boys, Andy made his way over to Ryan and asked if he wanted to play a card game. Surprised by the boy's sudden friendliness, Ryan agreed. Derrick joined them, while Rodney manned the boat. The three of them played cards for hours, laughing as they did, until the boat slowed down and Rodney pronounced, "We're here."

As the boat approached the shoreline, Ryan gazed at an endless white sanded pathway ahead. Nigel howled and wagged his tail in excitement while Ryan asked Andy where they were.

"We have reached the entrance," he replied.

As the boat neared the sand, Ryan saw the cave floor reappearing and continuing on into the distance. Once the boat could no longer move forward, Nigel jumped off the boat and into the shallow water. "Where's the entrance?" Ryan asked, glancing at the continuation of the cave.

Rodney grabbed the lantern and stepped off the boat. "We need to walk a little farther and we will be there."

As Ryan and the two other boys got off the boat, the cave began to tremble and a loud noise exploded in the air like a thunderous train rolling toward them. Noticing the trepidation in the faces of the boys, Ryan asked what was going on.

"They are breaking through!" yelled Rodney. "We have to run."

Nigel began to bark, and the boys sprinted ahead on the paved white sand, with Derrick now holding onto the lantern. Ryan, not expecting the full-on sprint, did not react at the same speed the boys did.

"What are you waiting for? They are coming, and we need to get you to the entrance!" shouted Andy as he looked back. As the noise surrounded him, Ryan dashed toward the boys. With each stride, the ground beneath Ryan shook and the noise raged on. They sprinted forward for what felt like an eternity to Ryan until suddenly the cave was silent once again.

Out of breath, Ryan stopped running, placed his hands on his knees, and asked, "Is it over?"

"It's just begun," Andy replied.

"Let's keep moving. We are almost there," Rodney said as they walked onward. Nigel continued his dash toward the entrance. As they walked side by side, the lantern light began to flicker as Derrick held on to it. The three boys stopped, turned to the light, and sighed, upset that it had been acting this way the entire day. They huddled together, trying to figure out why the lantern was behaving in such a manner.

As Ryan stood waiting for the boys to fix the lantern, he heard the whispering voice return: "Ryan, we're here." Following the voice, a gust of wind howled through the cave like a banshee. The boys turned to face the oncoming wind, and as they did, their eyes opened wide. Ryan noticed the change in their demeanor and looked back as well. What he saw heading in their direction was not something he had ever seen before—black smoke in the shape of snake-like creatures bursting in and out of the ground and the air.

"The light is not strong enough to hold them off! We have got to run—now!" shouted Rodney. With that, they all made a dash toward the entrance. Andy held onto the lantern, as the light flicked on and off.

Terrified to look back, Ryan could hear the whispering voice and the howling wind as he ran. In the distance, Nigel was barking at the oncoming danger, with his back side facing a beautiful waterfall that flowed into a clear, crystal blue lagoon. Racing ahead and nearing Nigel, Ryan watched as Andy fell down with the lantern in his hand. As the lantern hit the ground, the glass cracked, and light began to ooze out. The light in the cave began to dim.

"Ryan, you need to jump into the lagoon and swim to the other side. Without the light, we cannot hold them back!" Andy shouted as he attempted to stand up.

Ryan stopped running and turned around. He saw a black smoke creature shoot right through Andy's body, causing him to stumble. As he screamed out to Andy, Ryan felt Rodney and Derrick pushing him toward the water, telling him to let Andy be. Reluctantly, Ryan continued forward, taking one last glimpse back—what he saw were the creatures circling around Andy, eventually squeezing the life out of him. The most peculiar thing happened to Andy's lifeless body as it lay on the ground: it disintegrated into blue dust, which rose toward the ceiling. Turning back toward the lagoon, Ryan saw that he and the remaining two boys had reached their destination. Rodney, holding the broken lantern, which provided the dimmest of visibility, told Ryan it was time for him to go.

"Where am I going?" Ryan asked.

"You just have to trust me," replied Rodney. Just as Rodney spoke, the three of them were whipped to the ground by a burst of wind. Lying face down, Ryan pushed himself from the ground to sit up, trying to figure out what had happened. As he lifted his head up, he saw the creatures puffing in and out of the air, heading in his direction. As they neared, Ryan grabbed the lantern to have a better view of the oncoming danger. One of the creatures leaped towards him. The smoke nearing his face, Ryan placed the lantern light in front of the incoming foe, and when the light touched it, the creature let out a screeching noise, and an image of a man with razor-sharp teeth and a maddening look was visible inside the smoke. Following the noise, the creature disappeared.

Ryan quickly stood up, and Nigel raced to him, barking toward the water.

"Ryan, you have to jump in, swim down as far as you can, and go under the cave wall," Derrick said as he grabbed the lantern from Ryan's hand. "It's what you were brought here for. It's time to believe."

Absolutely dumbfounded, Ryan looked into the crystal blue water of the lagoon and asked the two boys if they were coming with him.

"This is not our journey. It's your time," said Rodney, looking anxious. "You will get all your answers later, but this is as far as we can go. Go now, and we will hold them off."

A nervous Ryan bent down to pet Nigel and said good-bye to the boys. Ryan jumped into the water and swam down. After swimming for what felt like an eternity, he turned his body to look up toward the surface. All he saw was Nigel staring down into the water.

CHAPTER 5

Hey, Champ

Ryan swam down through the clear blue water. He did not struggle at any point for air; it was as if he belonged in this beautiful undersea world. The water was teeming with life. There were multicolored fish, massive coral, sponges and plants. Eventually Ryan reached a fork in the cave. The water was split by a grey wall dividing two rooms, though the wall did not reach all the way to the bottom. Ryan swam toward the space between the floor and the wall, appreciating his surroundings and never fearing he would run out of breath. As he neared the wall, there were symbols and letters he had seen earlier carved into the bottom of the wall. In large letters, one word stood out: *INTRANT.* As he moved to the bottom of the wall, the Key in his pocket lit up. He touched the wall as he passed under it and went over to the opposite side.

When he came to the other side of the wall, Ryan began to swim up—the water was just as clear and wondrous. Light, however, was much more prevalent on this side—everything in the water illuminated. As his head emerged, he saw a waterfall coming out of the cave and plunging into the pool of water he was in. He swam toward the shallow end of the water and sat, the exhaustion hit him like a pile of bricks and his head pounded as he tried to sort out the events of his evening. Looking at his surroundings, he was still in the cave; however, now he saw white, powdery sand and a lavish amount of crystal blue waterfalls in the distance. Entranced by the beauty of the cave, he felt at ease. As he continued to analyze his surroundings Ryan couldn't find the source of the lighting in the cave; all of the walls appeared enclosed. Sitting in the water, he felt for the Key in his pocket, and a cold feeling spread throughout his body. His cell phone was in his pocket and was now saturated by the water. Sickness grasped him as he reached for his phone. The phone showed no signs of life. Ryan pressed the buttons, shook the phone frantically, and pounded it with his hands, but it would not turn on. "No. No, this can't be happening," Ryan muttered. Completely devastated, Ryan got out of the water, stepped onto the sand, and collapsed in agony.

Walking aimlessly through the hallways of Carrington Cray High School, Ryan looked disheveled from his hair to his clothes. He in no way wanted to be at school and was only there at the insistence of his mother. He walked through the doors and into the courtyard, where he sat down, placed his book bag and food on the table, and took his cell phone out of his pocket. He stared at the screen, which read, "One new voicemail"—the message his dad had left him two weeks before, on the day of the accident. Ryan hadn't been able to pull himself together and listen to it until that day.

"Hey Champ, I know we got in an argument today, but I just wanted to call and tell you how proud I am of you. There is so much in life a father has to teach his son. Don't ever forget that life will always throw obstacles in your way, but nothing can knock over what is built inside of you. I have seen what's inside of you, and that is greatness—greatness as a person and as a man. Champ, you are all I wanted in a child, and no one can ever take away the love I have for you. I love you, son."

Back in the cave, tears were running down Ryan's face as he realized that he had lost the last remnants of his dad's voice. Clutching his phone, he bent over and wept.

CHAPTER 6

Joe

Ryan heard a voice yelling out commands—he looked up. He saw a young man in his mid-twenties dressed in brown khaki pants and a white shirt, his hair combed perfectly to the side—this impeccably dressed man gave Ryan the impression he must have been in the military. The man was commanding ten to fifteen individuals, each of whom was carrying a bag. The group included men and women of all ages who were being led out of a side entrance of the cave. The young man was instructing them to follow a winding cobblestone path. The path was surrounded on both sides by gorgeous powdery white sand and waterfalls. The water fell down into crystal blue pools.

"Keep following the path, and in about thirty minutes, you will reach the First Post, where several guards will be awaiting your arrival," the young man said. As the group walked forward, a girl around Ryan's age caught his eye. He stared in amazement as she walked toward the cobblestone. With brown hair, a slender body, and a beautiful face, the girl was stunning.

Ryan, still sitting in the sand and clutching his cell phone, saw the young man staring at him. Unsure of what to do, he looked away. When he glanced back, the man was walking toward him.

"What are you doing moping around? I have been waiting for you here. Did you get lost on your way? Do you have the Key?"

Overwhelmed by the questions, Ryan looked at the man, confused. "Who are you, and where the heck are we?" Ryan asked as he felt frustration and anger arising.

At first, the young man looked displeased with Ryan's tone but quickly changed his demeanor and said, "Kid, my name is Joseph Smarrin, but my friends just call me Joe. As to where you are, we can discuss that on the way. Our travel will take time and we need to head out and follow the rest of the pack that just arrived." Joe extended his hand to Ryan and helped him off the ground.

"Why have you been waiting for me?" Ryan asked.

"I came here so that I can guide you," said Joe, as they began to walk toward the perfectly set cobblestone path.

As they began their trek down the path, Ryan explained to Joe what had happened to the boys. Joe's eyes widened and he whispered, "The Black Spirits made it through?!"

"What are you talking about?" Ryan asked.

"Did you see a type of smoke? If you did, those are the Black Spirits. They are just the beginning of it all—they must know you are here."

Frustrated, Ryan stopped walking and blurted out, "I am tired of all this vague talk. I need to know where I am and why I'm so important. All of this stuff going on can't be real."

Joe reached for Ryan's arm and pulled him forward. "You aren't ready to listen."

Ryan shoved Joe's arm off. "I'm done! You want me to keep walking? Then give me some real answers."

Joe agreed to Ryan's demand. "Let's go. We need to get to the First Post with the others, as there isn't much time. And by the way, I see the stories about you are true—you really are stubborn."

As they walked through their beautiful, serene surroundings, Ryan fired questions out to Joe. Ryan's first question regarded where they were headed.

"We are on our way to the Realm. It's a little bit of journey, and we need to pass three posts that have been set up so that anyone trying to get in is guided and protected on their way. That group up ahead is headed to the Realm."

"What's the Realm?" Ryan asked.

"The Realm is like nothing you have seen or visited before. It is a land that has been around for thousands of years, hiding but always in sight. I am one of the commanders of the Gate to the Realm. The Gatekeepers' job is to guard the entrance to the Realm."

These answers still did not leave Ryan satisfied. "Why was I led here?"

"Every so often, evil tries to enter the Realm to grab as many of us as they can and destroy everything we have built. In order for it to enter the Blue Alley—the passageway to the Realm, where we are now—it has to be as evil and dark as they come. The Black Spirits are part of an evil core known as the Devamans, who have always tried to find a way in to the Realm. No one knows where they live or where they come from, but it is believed to be a place of darkness and torment. For that reason, the Devamans' weakness is light, which is why we constantly have the Blue Alley lit up. The Black Spirits that you saw are always the first to show before a full attack by the Devamans. At the early stages, the Black Spirits are made mainly of black smoke; however, if they are able to move through the Blue Alley, they will begin to take some sort of human form. The strongest of all the Devamans is the Dark Shadow, who is the only one strong enough to lead an invasion into the Blue Alley. When a Dark Shadow rises, the Realm is always on high alert. We protect the Realm, but when a Dark Shadow is strong enough, the only way to make sure that the Realm is protected is with the Key. The Realm can only be truly secured from an attack when a specific Key is turned by someone not from the Realm. It is someone chosen, and that is you, Ryan. I was sent here to guide and protect you so you can turn that Key and save us, because evil is coming."

When Joe finished speaking, Ryan began to laugh out loud. "This sounds like a science fiction movie I've watched before. You really expect me to believe all of this garbage? I am no one. This Key was left on my door probably because it flew in from the storm. I am nothing special. I will follow you to the First Post only because I am starving and hope that there is food there. After that, please just show me the way back home." Joe agreed to Ryan's request and the two walked forward silently.

As they got closer to the group, Ryan counted thirteen members—eight men and five women. The ages ranged from eight to eighty. Now within talking distance, Joe asked for their attention and introduced Ryan. Reluctantly, Ryan said hi as they all waved hello. Ryan gave each of them a halfhearted smile—until he got to the girl.

"Ryan, this is Haley Landon."

Ryan stuttered for a moment until the words finally came out of his mouth. "Hi, I'm Ryan."

Haley, with her beautiful, yet sad face, responded, "Yeah, Joe just told us that."

Trying to get out of this daze, Ryan asked, "What are you doing in the Blue Alley?"

"I am trying to leave my home and go to the Realm, which I have been told is a much better place than where I'm from. My mom and two brothers are here too." She pointed to three people to his left.

"It's time to start moving again," Joe declared.

They continued their trek. Not wanting to leave Haley's side, Ryan asked if he could carry the strapped bag she was carrying.

"No," Haley said, "I was given this bag when I first started my journey to the Realm and was told that it contained extremely valuable items and should be opened only when I get there."

Ryan continued to try to make small talk with Haley, but she showed no interest. "I'm sorry. I don't have time to talk. I just want to walk with my family and make it inside. We so desperately need this."

Feeling rejected, Ryan complied with her request, went to the back of the group, and walked forward—unable to keep his eyes off Haley Landon.

CHAPTER 7

The First Post

Just as Ryan thought he could walk no further, Joe finally announced, "We are reaching the First Post."

In the distance, Ryan saw two large, gray pillars. As he moved closer, he could see the pillars were about twenty-five feet high, with a wood door at the bottom connected to the pillars. Linked on the back side of the pillars was a white brick fortress. The Roman numerical number one was engraved at the top of the door, and once again, all of the symbols and images he had seen throughout his journey reappeared. On top of the door was a white brick wall connecting the front of the pillars. This wall had a circular ring in the middle, which provided the glow that lit up the Blue Alley. Guarding the entrance were two men dressed similar to Joe. When they saw Joe, they made a hand gesture and began to open the door. As the door opened, the word *"Fides"* was seen carved into the pillars. The carving began to shine as they neared. Passing the two guards, the group entered the First Post.

"Dad, what happens when I fall asleep? How do I know I will wake up?" a twelve-year-old Ryan asked from a hospital bed, his right arm in a sling.

Pulling the chair close to his son, Ryan's dad whispered in his ear, "Because you're going to. You have so much waiting for you when you do."

At that moment, Ryan felt more at ease. He grabbed his father's hand and said, "Dad, I did everything you told me to do out there on the field. The batter hit a long fly ball all the way to the end of the street. I kept my eyes on the ball the entire time, and at the last second, I turned around and *wham!* I hit a street sign."

Trying to hold back from laughing, his dad bit his lip and asked, "So did you catch the ball?"

Ryan stared blankly at his father. "I can't remember."

The two burst out in laughter as his father jokingly said he'd better have caught it. The two of them talked for an hour about everything in Ryan's life from school to girls to movies until a nurse came in and told Ryan it was time to go. He was wheeled out of the hospital room and down the hallway through the double doors where his surgery would take place. As they wheeled him, his dad held his hand, and before he went into the operation room, Ryan said, "Thanks, Dad." With his mind at peace, Ryan went into the unknown.

As they made their way into the First Post, the cobblestone path continued in a straight line. Inside the post were two one-story, light blue buildings. Both buildings—one to Ryan's right and one to his left—contained the same foreign symbols and images. As Ryan looked ahead, he noted the cobblestone path eventually led to a small bridge, which passed through a beautiful waterfall. The water from the waterfall fell down gracefully onto the bridge and into a moat that circled the waterfall.

"Okay, let's stop for a few minutes," Joe stated. "I am sure you are all hungry and thirsty. I will go grab each of you some bread and water." The group walked over to several benches that were by the blue building to their left and placed their bags under their legs— making sure no one took them. Ryan glanced over to Haley and saw her looking in his direction. Once she spotted his gaze she quickly turned to speak to her family. Ryan looked to his left, and saw Joe walking to the door of one of the buildings, and decided to follow.

Joe, paying no attention to Ryan, reached for the door and entered the blue building. As Ryan neared the door, one of the words carved into the walls, *"Reflexio,"* lit up. Unsure of what he was walking into, he opened the door with caution, making sure not to disturb whatever or whoever was inside. He took a few steps in before a guard appeared.

"What are you doing here? You aren't supposed to be in here," the guard stated angrily.

As the guard pushed him away, Ryan was able to catch a glimpse of the inside. There were silver sconces with candles mounted on the walls of the building. The lighting in the room was dim; however he did see several individuals sitting on a row of benches. Ryan did not have enough time to make out much of what they were doing.

"Thanks, Carl, for keeping an eye on him. I'll take it from here," said Joe, patting the guard on the back. Joe, with a bag of water and bread in his hands, asked Ryan to follow him. "Help me pass out the bread," Joe said. They walked back to the group, and Joe began to pass out the water. Before passing out the bread, Ryan grabbed a piece of bread and ate it—Joe stared condescendingly. Annoyed, Ryan grabbed the bread and began to hand out pieces to the group. He finally got to Haley and her family. As he was about to hand the bread to them, a loud, ringing alarm was heard. Ryan looked over to the front entrance and saw a blinking red light.

"What is going on, Joe?" Ryan asked.

Joe moved quickly to the other building and yelled out, "A new group has arrived!"

Scurrying out of the building, Ryan watched as Joe put small blue crystals into his pocket and called over two of the guards, who were carrying camping bags. One of the guards gave his bag to Joe. Anxious to find out what was going on, Ryan strode over to where the three of them were. As the alarm discontinued, he asked, "Joe, is everything okay?"

Surprised to see Ryan by his side, Joe replied, "Yes, that alarm is just letting us know that a new group is ready to enter the Blue Alley. The job of the guards here at the First Post is to make sure the new group is safely placed onto the path toward the Realm. If you still want to go back home, come with us to pick them up, and then I will show you the way back."

Relieved at the thought of going home, Ryan nodded. Joe told the guard, Carl, and another guard he referred to as "John," that he would meet them at the front entrance of the First Post. The two guards agreed and walked toward the front, and Joe went over to the group, which were huddled around the benches. When the members of the group saw him coming, they stood up, with their bags in their hands.

"Listen. All you have to do is continue down the path to the next two posts, and you will then enter the Realm. There will be guards stationed throughout your journey who will assist you." The group members exchanged confused looks at each other, unsure of what to do. A man who looked to be in his mid-sixties asked, "Will we be safe on our own?"

"Nothing to fear, my friend. Nothing to fear," Joe firmly responded.

Moving toward the path, each member of the group thanked Joe for his help. Ryan scanned the crowd for Haley and saw her and her mother arguing as her two brothers tried to interject. Though her mom was losing her cool, Haley, so beautiful and confident, kept her composure and said, "Mother, he may be in this group that just arrived. I must go with Joe. If he is there, he will be all alone and I can bring him back to us safely."

Her mother shook her head. "What if you get lost?"

"Mother, I can take care of myself." Haley called over her brothers and said, "Dan, Eric, we are so close to getting there, so just keep going, and take Mom with you. I will be right behind you."

Eric tried to convince Haley to go with them, but she dismissed him. As Ryan continued to stare in their direction, he noticed that

Eric appeared to be the older of the two brothers. He was tall and skinny and had short brown hair, while Dan was about Ryan's age and smaller in stature. Tired of arguing, Haley's mother gave in and embraced Haley in a lengthy hug. With tears running down her face, Haley's mom grabbed the two boys' arms and walked along the path toward the waterfall.

Fighting off her own tears, Haley called out to Joe and asked him if she could come along. At first, he was hesitant, but with Haley's insistence, he eventually agreed. Joe grabbed his bag, placed it around his arms, and told Haley and Ryan to follow him.

As they moved toward the exit of the First Post, both Haley and Ryan turned to look back at what they were leaving behind. Haley turned to wave good-bye to her family. Knowing he would be going home, Ryan glanced back to catch one last glimpse of this bizarre reality he had landed in. As he stared back, a man and woman in their forties who were part of the group they had arrived with came to see Joe. Their faces exhibited nervousness and uncertainty as to what to do next. The woman blurted out to Joe, "We are not ready to go by ourselves to the Realm. What should we do?"

Joe pointed to the blue buildings and said, "That's what these are here for."

His response brought tranquility to the couple and they went to the door of the light blue building to their left. Ryan watched as they entered. He then saw the rest of the group members in the distance at a standstill on the bridge. As they were about to be engulfed by the waterfall flowing on top of the bridge, the water suddenly ceased flowing down, and the path ahead of them was cleared. Stunned, he turned toward Haley to see if she had witnessed the same thing, but she was walking with a purpose toward the entrance. At that moment, Ryan looked back to see if what he had seen was real, but the group was already gone, and the water was once again rolling over the bridge.

In front of the entrance, Ryan, Joe, and Haley met up with John and Carl. Joe gave the two guards a nod to proceed, and the five of them headed back to the serene sand and waterfalls of the Blue Alley.

At that moment, Ryan thought of the last time he was at the beach with his parents. He was sixteen years old and had gotten into his rebellious teenage years. At that point in his life, he'd wanted to be independent, never liked being told what to do, and just wanted to hang out with his friends. They were staying at a nearby beach called Manro Island for a four-day vacation, and all his friends were there with their families. Ryan had spent the entire time with his friends in the "family vacation" and with one day left, his father asked if he would go play golf with him. With some urging from his mother, he reluctantly agreed and said he would meet up with his father at 2:30 p.m. after spending the morning at the beach with his friends. That day, time flew by, as Ryan and his friends played football in the water and spoke to any girl who passed by. Eventually, he asked a friend what time it was. It was 3:00 p.m. At that moment, instead of calling his father, Ryan continued to have fun with his friends, forgetting his promise. That night, when he got back, his mother told him how hurt his father was and how he had waited for over an hour.

As Ryan thought back on that day, he was filled with regret. This feeling had consumed Ryan's heart and mind ever since his father passed away. Days, weeks, and months passed after his father's death, and all Ryan could think about was all the things he wished he'd done differently. He would have helped his father fix the lights on the roof at home, gone with his dad to run his errands when he asked, seen the movies he'd wanted to see—the list went on and on in Ryan's head. This guilt left no room for anything else. His passion for baseball, the enjoyment in hanging out with his friends, the excitement in looking at different universities was all gone. He was lost in life and could not find his way back.

CHAPTER 8

Haley

As Joe announced they were ten minutes away from the pickup station, Ryan could not soak in his beautiful surroundings. He was too focused on the pain and anger inside. However, every time he gazed over at Haley, a flicker of hope seemed to enter his body. As they walked, John and Carl led the way, followed by Joe, Ryan, and Haley. Ryan decided to take another chance and strike up a conversation with Haley.

"Can I ask you something?" Ryan said.

She turned to Ryan and nodded. Her green eyes mesmerized him.

"Why did you leave your family to come with us?"

As Ryan stared into her gorgeous eyes, Haley opened up to him and divulged the story of how she ended up at the Blue Alley. "My family and I come from a poor neighborhood where every day is a struggle. My mom worked two jobs, and I worked as a waitress after school every day just to make sure we had enough food on the table for me, my mom, and my three brothers. Since we lived in a poor area, the schools my brothers and I went to were awful. We were surrounded by drugs, gangs, and violence. My brother Dan was always a troublemaker and was always in conflicts at school. Eric is so bright but he's such a follower and wants desperately to be like Dan, even though he is the older brother.

"Then there is my poor Dylan, my little brother, who is now ten years old. He was in an elementary school where the books were outdated and the classrooms were covered in dust. So after my senior year of high school, with my mother unable to afford college, I began to work full-time—until the other day, when a man offered me 'the chance of a lifetime,' as he put it. The man showed me pamphlets and pictures of this placed called the Realm, where he said my family and I would be taken care of at no cost. 'A life without worries,' he said. The pictures he showed of this place were stunning. But of course, this all sounded too good to be true, so I told the man, who was dressed in a beautiful navy suit, that I was not going to fall for his scam. The man, whose name was Rodger, was not upset at my decision, and he simply said he would be back in a couple of days to see if I had changed my mind. I tried to research "the Realm" on the internet but all found was information on some video game.

"So a couple days passed, and sure enough, he came back to the diner during one of my night shifts. Except this time, I was willing to listen to his sales pitch, as two days earlier, my brother Dylan had been badly beaten on his way home from school by kids three years older than him. At that point, I knew it was time for a change. So when Rodger came and spoke of this place with such conviction, I told him we were in. He gave me this bag that I am holding now and told me to be at the local ferry the following day by 4:00 p.m. He went on to tell me that he would make sure that my mom and brothers would be there as well.

"I showed up at the ferry dock at 3:50 p.m., and there was my mom with Eric and Dan, each with their own bag. But there was no sign of Dylan. When the ferry horn sounded for its departure and everyone was told to board, I panicked. I had just started to take steps to get off the ferry when Rodger appeared and told me not to worry, that he was on his way to pick up Dylan, who would be placed on the next ferry and would meet us in the Realm. The reassurance and confidence in his voice helped me to relax. So as we left on the ferry, I saw Rodger leave the port in his car to go pick up Dylan. Once the ferry arrived, we got off with the others and made our way here, and that is when we first met Joe and saw you."

"So you're hoping that the group coming in now is the ferry that would bring your brother Dylan?" he asked.

"Yes."

Before Ryan could ask his next question, Carl and John stopped in their tracks, causing Ryan and Haley to bump into them.

"Why did you stop?" Ryan asked.

"Because we arrived at our destination," Joe emphatically stated.

Ryan glanced to his right and saw two waterfalls with a navy blue sand path directly between them. The path veered off to the right of the cobblestone. Carl and John once again led the way.

"Joe, you said you would show me the way back home once we got here. And we are here," Ryan stated.

With a stoic face, Joe turned to Ryan and told him that once they got the new group into the Blue Alley, he would gladly show him the way back home. Annoyed by his response, Ryan agreed. The five of them pressed on, following the new path. As they passed between the two waterfalls, Ryan looked to the left, and out of the corner of his eye, he saw what looked like a decrepit body in the water, its face partially filled with flesh and the rest of bone. As he stared in horror at this image, the whispering voice returned, calling his name once again.

Ryan couldn't take his eyes off the figure. The whispering voice continued until the body in the water raised one of its hands and pointed a finger at Ryan.

"Let's go. What are you waiting for?" Joe asked, placing his hands on Ryan and awakening him from his trance. "The quicker we move, the quicker you'll get home."

Still reeling from what he'd seen, Ryan asked Carl if he had heard or seen anything.

"If there was a noise, I would have heard it," Carl said as he continued forward.

Trying to shake the horrifying image from his mind, Ryan quickly moved ahead. As they passed the waterfalls, he saw a set of stairs leading down. Looking down the staircase, the light, which was so bright in the Blue Alley, did not completely flow down the steps.

"What is down there?" Ryan asked.

"That is where we pick up the new group, which should arrive any minute now," Carl excitedly proclaimed. And with that, a horn from a ferry could be heard coming from down below. Like two excited children on Christmas, Carl and John ran down the stairs.

CHAPTER 9

The Drop-Off Point

As they reached the bottom of the staircase, the visibility in the cave decreased. The main source of light derived from the Blue Alley above the stairs. The staircase connected to a dock, and the surrounding water steered out to an opening in the cave—leading out to an immense body of water. The docking station was filled with fog. As Ryan observed his surroundings, the siren from the ferry sounded once, and the water inside the cave began to sway. Looking toward the opening in the cave, Ryan saw lights appear as the ferry made its way through the fog. With the ferry drawing near, Ryan looked back at Haley, whose face was full of anticipation and hope.

The wave swells began to subside as the ferry slowed its motion, and Ryan saw the two-story ferry and its 1980s-style appearance. Although old in style, the blue and white ferry was in great condition. In blue lettering, the name of the boat emerged into sight: *"Fatum."* Staring at the ferry, Ryan realized it was the same boat he had seen in the pictures from the shed.

Nearing the dock, the ferry slowed further and, eventually crept to a halt. As the engine shut down, a ferry worker opened the door of the boat and pulled out a small gray bridge to connect the ferry to the dock. Joe strolled over to speak with the worker and asked how many passengers were on board.

"There are only seven today, Joe," said the worker as the passengers with their bags in their hand prepared to exit. As they did, Joe began providing instructions.

"Welcome, everyone. Welcome to the Blue Alley. My name is Joe, and I, along with John and Carl, will be guiding you to your ultimate destination. We are excited to have each one of you here, and I am sure you are all anxious to get to the Realm. So let's get going."

The passengers began to disembark from the ferry. Watching the passengers, Ryan saw the first two to get off were a young woman, in her mid-thirties, and her young son, whom Ryan assumed was seven. Two young men around Ryan's age followed, laughing. As they walked by Ryan, he looked over at Haley, who grew tenser with each passenger. The final three passengers walked off. Dylan was not one of them. Instead, they were two men and one woman in their mid-forties. These three walked off the ferry, and unlike the others, who were excited, their demeanor was serious as they passed Ryan, staring at him.

"I am so sorry, Haley," Ryan said sincerely. "Maybe he will be on the next one or is already in the Realm."

As the ferry pushed off the dock and headed out, Haley ran toward it and yelled out, "Are you sure there is no one left? My brother should have been on board." The ferry worker looked at her and apologized, saying only he and the captain remained.

Tears began streaming down her face and she gave Ryan a hug, which caught him off guard. Feeling like he never wanted her to let go, he whispered out, "Everything will be okay, Haley."

Absolutely dejected, Haley pushed away from Ryan, stormed passed everyone and walked up the stairs, alone.

Feeling Haley's pain as if it were his own, Ryan walked toward the stairs to follow her, but Joe grabbed his arm. "Ryan, let her go. She will be okay. There is nothing for you to do."

Ryan shrugged off Joe's hand and kept moving forward. As he passed the new arrivals, who were awaiting further commands from Joe, the last three passengers to walk off the ferry blocked off Ryan's way.

"Could you please move?" Ryan asked politely.

"No we can't, kid," said the portly gentleman to Ryan's right. The man was dressed in a worn-out polo shirt and faded jeans. He looked at the man to Ryan's left and said, "Hey, Lumond, this kid wants me to move. What do you think I should do?"

Lumond, laughed out loud, "No Harry, we should let him go when we feel like it." Lumond, who was of medium size and dressed in khaki shorts and a fishing shirt, yelled out, "Lorrie, stay right where you are."

The poorly dressed woman, Lorrie, who stood between the two men, was diminutive in stature with frizzy hair and crooked teeth. She burst into laughter as well. Fuming, Ryan gave a hard shove to Harry's chest. Lumond grabbed Ryan by the arms, and right before Harry came in with a fist to Ryan's stomach, Joe yelled out, "What is the problem here?"

Joe, his face serious and his fist clenched, eased up when Lumond let go of Ryan.

"We were just having a little fun with our buddy over here," said Harry, as he rubbed Ryan's head condescendingly. Ryan immediately turned around and straightened up, ready to fight, until Joe pulled him aside. "Bye, sweetie," said Lorrie. The three erupted into laughter as Joe and Ryan walked up the stairs.

"I didn't need your help," he angrily proclaimed to Joe as they went up toward the Blue Alley.

"Why are you so angry? You need to harness the anger inside and let go," Joe responded. Ryan ignored Joe, his thoughts wandered to a fight he'd gotten into two weeks after his father had passed. It was his second day back at school, and he was walking down a hallway, lost in a daze. As he was walking, another student accidentally bumped into him, causing the watch his father had given him, to fall to the floor. Seeing the watch on the floor, made Ryan snap. He pushed the boy into the lockers, and swung his arms violently towards the boy, until students were able to pry Ryan away.

Once Ryan reached the top of the stairs, he saw Haley on the ground crying, and all the anger inside of him vanished for the moment. As he reached her, he expressed how sorry he was for her pain and told her he would help her find her brother.

"I thought you wanted to go home," she said as she looked at him, her green eyes filled with tears. He told her that he would go home only after they found her brother. And with that, Ryan saw Haley smile for the first time.

CHAPTER 10

Darkness Arrives

Ryan and Haley walked together past the waterfalls and out to the Blue Alley with all of its flowing water and captivating sand. The two waited there for several minutes as the rest of the group made their way toward them. As John and Carl, the last ones up, reached the rest of the group, Haley noticed an unusual look on Ryan's face and asked him what was wrong.

"Joe," Ryan stuttered. "Is that normal?" He pointed toward one of the waterfalls. The eyes of the entire group followed Ryan's hand and saw that the water flowing down was red.

"Joe, is this the Devamans?" John asked.

All eyes were focused on the waterfall—red now dominating the water.

"I've never seen this happen before," Joe muttered.

And with that, the waterfalls all around the Blue Alley began to spew red.

"What the heck is going on here?" shouted Harry. "You bring us to this place, and you promise us paradise, and now we have red freaking water."

Wanting to see it up close, John began to walk over to the waterfall near them.

"What are you doing, man?" shouted Lumond.

"I am trying to see what is going on," said John.

"Okay, let's start walking and get to the First Post as quickly as possible," Joe calmly spoke.

Just as he finished speaking, a loud noise like a car alarm blared loudly, and the light in the Blue Alley began to flicker.

"This can't be good," Carl whispered. "Joe, I thought that the lighting could not be affected."

Joe replied, "There are only a few who know how the lighting works. Let's all stay together."

Trying to figure out what was going on; Ryan looked around to see where everybody was. In the flickering light, Ryan saw the young boy holding onto his mother's leg for dear life as his mother tried to comfort him. The two young men had their eyes wide open and were looking around. Lumond, Harry, and Lorrie were whispering to each other, showing little emotion. Joe and Carl huddled together— sifting through their bags.

Ryan looked at Haley—she was mumbling something under her breath. Her face was pale as she stared right at a waterfall. With the alarm continuing and the light fading in and out of the Blue Alley, Ryan walked over to her.

"What is it, Haley? What are you saying?" Ryan asked.

She kept muttering the same words, and finally he figured it out: "They took him. He is gone."

"Who did they take?" he asked.

"John!" Haley shouted.

All of a sudden, utter silence and darkness over took the Blue Alley. The serene sound of water flowing down was no longer heard in the obscurity.

"Ryan," the whispering voice called.

Ryan tried to look around but could see nothing. He only heard the voices of desperation shouting out around him.

"I can't see anything!"

"Where is everyone?"

"What do we do?"

Once again, Joe spoke out calmly. "Everyone needs to quiet down."

"You guys are a joke," an annoyed Lorrie replied. "You promise all this perfection and beautiful this and that—and now look at us. We are in darkness."

This was met with agreement from Lumond and Harry.

Ignoring the complaints, Joe continued speaking. "Give me a moment, and I will get us some light."

Ryan felt a gust of wind on the back of his neck.

"It's the black spirits. They are here," Carl said nervously. He called out to John, who did not respond.

"What was that?" Haley shouted. "Something just moved under my feet."

The anxiety and tension within the group began to thicken as the wind swirled all around. The young boy begged his mom to make it stop.

"Ryan, there is no escape," said the whispering voice.

Ryan asked Haley if she heard the voice, but she said no—all she heard was a howling wind.

"Joe, you have got to get us out of here!" shouted Ryan. And with that, a glow emerged from an object in Joe's hand—it was a diminutive yellow fluorescent container.

"Get ready to go when I say so. This is going to buy us about ten minutes, so make sure you sprint," Joe stated. He pulled back the arm holding the container, clicked a button on the top to turn off the glow, and threw the container in the direction of the entrance to the Blue Alley. Darkness surrounding them on all sides, a ticking sound could be heard. With a sound like a transformer turning on, light began to appear in the distance. The light crept closer and closer to the group until it reached them and continued moving towards the First Post. "Run!" shouted Joe.

Carl led the group forward, with the two young men from the new arrivals running right behind him. Ryan and Haley followed, and Joe stayed in the back to protect the mother, who was carrying her son as she ran. Harry, Lorrie, and Lumond sprinted passed the group and ran on their own towards the First Post. As the group raced onward, Ryan looked up and saw at the top of the Blue Alley, the snake-like creatures moving in tandem through the cave wall.

"Joe, behind you—there is something there!" Haley yelled out. The ground was swelling as if a creature was plowing through the sand.

"They can't reveal themselves as long as we have the light. We have to make it to the post before it runs out," yelled Joe.

Ryan looked back and saw the young mother struggling with her son. At that instant, Ryan thought of the times he and his dad had taken the train to go see a basketball game. The trains would be full, and Ryan's father would always give up his seat to a woman or child who was standing up. "Son, always make sure to protect woman and children and those who are weaker than you."

"What are you doing, Ryan?" Haley yelled out to Ryan. Slowing his pace, he grabbed the boy from the mom's grasp. "I will take him. You won't make it at this pace." The boy, with tears in his eyes, told his mom that it was all right as the woman pleaded with Ryan to take care of her son.

"We have to move faster, guys," Joe proclaimed as the ground swelled up behind them. With the boy in Ryan's arms, the sprint was on. "What's your name, kid?" he asked as he ran.

All tense and nervous, the boy said with a stutter, "My—my name is Cooper."

"Okay, Cooper. Just hold on tight and we will be all right," Ryan panted as they continued to run. The light from Joe's container illuminated the view of the cobblestone path toward the First Post.

"We are about ten minutes away. Don't let up!" Joe shouted.

The group began to lose some steam as exhaustion crept in. Suddenly, the wind, the noises, the ground swelling behind them, and the snake-like creatures above were gone. One of the young men slowed down and said he needed a breather.

"We can't stop. We are so close," Joe said as he continued his pace with no shortness of breath or noticeable exhaustion.

"Come on, Joe, we are all about to collapse here," Ryan sputtered, his body feeling the pain of carrying Cooper. "The Devamans are gone. We can take a quick break."

As Ryan's words came out of his mouth, and the rest of the group stopped running—a large sink hole came into view. The hole broke the cobblestone path ahead. As they neared it, Lorrie and Harry were seen screaming down into the hole.

"Thank goodness you guys are here," Harry said "We really could use your help. We were walking when all of a sudden the ground exploded under us and Lumond fell into the hole. It's about ten feet deep, and we can't get him out."

Ryan rolled his eyes at the change in Harry's tone.

"We lost you guys over there and were trying to look for you," said Lorrie.

Ryan was ready to keep walking and leave the three to fend for themselves when he noticed Joe looking through his bag. He pulled out a lengthy white rope. "Joe, don't we need to keep going? The light is going to run out," said Carl.

"Our job is to protect anyone who wants to enter the Realm. We can't leave anyone behind," Joe said softly.

With a dark sinister look, Harry stared at Carl. Joe and Harry lowered the rope into the hole as Lumond yelled out, "What is taking you guys so long?" In the meantime, Cooper left Ryan's arms and went to his mother, and Carl gave water to the two young men, who introduced themselves as Tarien and James. As they waited for Lumond to be pulled out, Ryan observed Carl looking over his shoulders—making sure the enemy was gone.

CHAPTER 11

Perimeters

Joe and Harry were able to pull Lumond out. As they did, a wounded and ungrateful Lumond griped over the amount of time it had taken; then, without a moment's notice, a beeping sound could be heard in the distance.

"No! No! I thought we had more time," Carl shouted out.

"What is that?" Haley asked.

Joe, began pulling materials out of his bag, and replied, "It's about to go dark again."

"What do you mean?" Haley sputtered out frantically.

"It means we have run out of time to make it to the First Post. I only had one container, and it's about to run out."

The group began to panic and ask questions as the beeping from the container continued. Lorrie, Harry, and Lumond cursed out loud, while Cooper could be seen comforting his mother.

Calmly, Joe whispered, "Carl, set up the perimeter on all four sides."

Following the command, Carl reached into his bag and grabbed four gray metal cylinders with a blue top at the tip of each one. "Everyone stay inside the cylinders," Joe stated.

"What are those for?" Ryan asked.

"To save us," Joe replied.

As Ryan gazed out in the direction of the First Post, Carl placed the first cylinder so it pointed in the direction of the hole and the First Post, the second toward the waterfalls to their right, the third in the direction of the entrance to the Blue Alley and the fourth to the waterfalls to their left.

As they all huddled within the cylinders, the beeping from the container began to slow its pace. The pauses between the beeps grew longer until one last beep sounded. The light in the Blue Alley began to be slowly drawn back into the container from all angles. As it did, the cave lighting dimmed, and darkness eventually fell upon the Blue Alley. Shortly after, a small fluorescent light providing minimal visibility appeared in the middle of the perimeter as Joe placed a thin, blue glowing pole into the ground.

The Blue Alley was eerily silent—the only noise heard were the breaths of the group. Suddenly, the cylinder facing the entrance of the Blue Alley shot out a bright silver light in the shape of a thin silver dome—zooming through the air, lighting up each area it passed.

"What was that?" asked James.

"That, James, tells us when we are not alone," whispered Carl.

As the light from the cylinder faded away, everyone huddled closer together.

"What do you mean we're not alone?" shouted Harry. "Who in the world is out there that we are so afraid of?"

Joe, trying to get Harry to keep his voice down, was interrupted as the cylinder facing the waterfalls to their right and the First Post shot out the silver light. This was followed by another surge of light toward the waterfalls on their left.

"Good going!" James whispered to Harry, upset.

As more shots of light burst out from the cylinders, Ryan came close to Haley, Cooper, and his mom. "Ryan, it's no use. Join us," said the reemerging whispering voice. His heart beat rapidly and sweat dripped down his face. Ryan looked around, but he could not see much. As the cylinders ceased firing, a noise came from each of them, as they shook, building up a yellow light inside them that dove straight down into the ground. The yellow light lit up the ground around them and connected each one of the cylinders—it was a diamond web of light.

"Joe, what is that?" whispered Ryan.

"That's so the Black Spirits can't enter the perimeter from underground. We are safe here until the next group of guards from the First Post come looking for us."

The wind and noises in the Blue Alley returned. From all over, Ryan could hear the ground cracking and the walls crumbling.

"Stay together," Joe commanded. As he looked toward the First Post, the ground swelled up, and the cylinder facing that direction shot out light like a canon. As it did, a Black Spirit emerged from the ground. Just as quickly, the spirit disappeared into thin air before reappearing closer to the group, shrieking. A second black spirit emerged right behind the first; however, the light crashed into the Black Spirits and crushed right through them. With a squeal, they exploded into black dust—falling down to the ground.

"Did you see the faces in the smoke creatures?" Tarien whispered, terrified. "It looked like half-eaten humans were stuck inside them."

At once, the Black Spirits came at them from all directions. Simultaneously, the cylinders began firing off light in response. Howling and screeching came from the creatures. Despite the chaos, Joe was calm as ever, telling everyone to stay away from the outside of the perimeter. "They will not be able to penetrate in here," he said.

As the silver lights zoomed through the air in each direction, the Black Spirits appeared in and out of thin air like night crawlers, but once they barreled into the blazing light from the cylinders, they quickly evaporated to the ground.

"We have this covered," said Harry. "They are getting destroyed."

As if they had understood Harry, the Black Spirits vanished, and with a crackling noise, they began to plow through the ground toward the perimeter.

"Are we safe?" Haley said. "They're coming at us from underground."

"The cylinders are impenetrable," Carl whispered to Haley.

"Here they come!" shouted Tarien.

A rumbling sound came from the ground as the creatures barreled through the sand towards them. "Move closer to Haley and me," Ryan told Cooper and his mom. Meanwhile, Ryan could hear Lorrie, Harry, and Lumond complaining of their current predicament. Ryan peered over at Joe and saw that he and Carl were kneeling down and whispering.

As the Black Spirits plowed closer and the noise from the ground grew more intense, James shouted, "This it. They are here!"

The Black Spirits nearing, Ryan reached for Haley's hand. She squeezed his hand anticipating the worst. There was suddenly a loud thud followed by squealing sounds coming from the Black Spirits, as the cylinders shot light down through the ground—vaporizing the creatures as they tried to penetrate the perimeter. Wanting to see what was happening, Tarien walked toward the middle of the two cylinders facing the entrance of the Blue Alley, and as he got closer, a Black Spirit burst out from the ground. As it did, the cylinders created a silver shield that lifted upward, blocking the Black Spirit from entering. Staring at the Black Spirit, Tarien could see a decrepit human body with skeletal features covered by thick black smoke. As everyone gazed at the Black Spirit, it disappeared and everything became quiet. The group rejoiced.

"Are they gone?" asked Haley.

Ryan and Haley became aware they were still holding hands and exchanged smiles, as they let go. With silence all around, and the wind calm, the group talked out loud to one another. Ryan and Haley introduced themselves to Tarien, James, and Cooper's mother. Ryan looked over to Carl and Joe, who were whispering to each other and searching through their bags. They each grabbed blue crystals, put them into smaller bags and placed them in their pockets.

Ryan walked over to Joe. "Are we going to head out?"

"Not yet. We need to wait a little longer to make sure that we are safe," said Joe.

Before walking to Haley and the rest of the group, Ryan asked about something that was bothering him. "Joe, who would have deliberately sabotaged the lighting in the Blue Alley?"

With a blank look on his face, Joe replied, "I don't know, but someone or something is out there that knows too much."

CHAPTER 12

What Awaits Underground

"I'm done waiting around!" Harry shouted when told they had to stay a while longer within the perimeter.

"Just wait a few more minutes so we can be sure the Black Spirits are gone," Joe replied.

Lumond, Lorrie and Harry unwilling to listen, grabbed their bags.

"Don't go past the perimeter yet. It is too dark out there!" Carl shouted.

But they would not listen. Trying to help, Ryan grabbed Harry's shoulder and asked him to remain inside the cylinders. Harry turned around, enraged, and yelled at Ryan.

In the meantime, Lumond and Lorrie continued to move toward the perimeter that faced the hole in the cobblestone. Joe and Carl, preoccupied with keeping Harry and Ryan from brawling, were unable to see Lumond and Lorrie venture outside of the perimeter, into the darkness, and toward the right side of the hole. As they strolled out, they passed the hole to their left and continued in the direction of the First Post for about twenty-five feet, until a light rocketed out of a cylinder in the direction of Lumond and Lorrie.

The group collectively turned around, as the light raced toward them.

"The light will not affect them," Carl said, "It only affects the Black Spirits." Carl was proved right as the light passed through Lumond and Lorrie, causing them no harm. The group shouted out for them to run back into the perimeter. Lumond and Lorrie turned to look behind them and with faces of fear sprinted towards the group. A Black Spirit had appeared a couple of feet behind them, causing a light to rupture out of the cylinder toward the Black Spirit.

"Run! Faster!" Harry yelled.

The light whizzed toward the Black Spirit, about to collide into it, the Black Spirit split in two and disappeared, only to reappear a moment later and blast through Lumond.

"No!" yelled Lorrie, as she made it back into the perimeter.

The group stared as the Black Spirit dragged Lumond's body into the hole. As he fell in, buzzing sounds came from the hole and the sand began to swell, in all directions, as the Black Spirits plowed through the ground toward the hole.

"Everyone, stay inside the perimeter," Joe shouted.

"They planned this!" Carl said in horror.

Standing close together, they watched as the hole began to move in a circular motion, as hundreds of Black Spirits gathered inside plowing through the soil. As they gained speed, the terrain around the perimeter began to rattle, and the hole began to grow. The movement of the hole gained steam as the ground rumbled. The cylinder facing the hole shook and eventually became dislodged and rolled towards the hole. With the perimeter now down, there was nothing to prevent the Black Spirits from entering.

Ferociously, the Black Spirits moved the hole toward the group. The group panicked, as the screeching noise grew higher in pitch. Out of the corner of his eye, Ryan saw a black tentacle appear from the hole—grabbing onto the right leg of Lorrie. The tentacle, scaly and slimy, had three claws at the end which locked onto Lorrie's ankle, causing her to fall. Seeing Lorrie being dragged toward the hole, Joe leaped forward and grabbed her hand. As he held on tight, his body began to be pulled in as well.

"Don't you let go of me," barked out Lorrie. "Don't you dare!"

In the blink of an eye, a Black Spirit appeared and crashed into Lorrie's back. Still breathing, Lorrie lay on the ground as two more Black Spirits swarmed around her. She let go of Joe, screaming, and was tossed into the hole.

"We have to go—now!" Joe yelled as he picked himself up from the ground. In a mad scramble, everyone grabbed their bags, and as the hole continued to swirl and the Black Spirits swarmed all around, Joe gave Ryan the bag of blue crystals. "Use it when you run out of options," Joe instructed.

As they began to run toward the First Post, Haley screamed out. Turning around, Ryan saw Haley being dragged by a black tentacle which had emerged from the hole—what the tentacles were connected to was not seen.

"Haley!" he yelled, dashing to help her.

"Joe, help!" he shouted as he grabbed her arm. "Don't you dare let go, Haley. We haven't even found your brother yet."

Haley yelled in agony as the claws from the tentacles pierced through her ankle. Meanwhile, Joe rummaged through his bag. "Joe, we have more trouble on the way," Ryan said, motioning with his head to the Black Spirits, who were headed in their direction. Joe quickly grabbed out of his bag a twenty-inch thin, white, steel blade. As he held onto the brown handle of the blade, a bright radiance surrounded it.

"Move out of the way!" he yelled to Ryan. Joe leapt into the air and sliced the tentacle in half, as the light from the blade seared right through it.

Before Ryan could sigh, two Black Spirits appeared and grabbed hold of Haley. They wrapped around her like a snake squeezing its prey. As Haley gasped for air, Ryan went to help but was tossed down by a Black Spirit who had emerged from the ground.

"Joe, save her!" Ryan shouted as he hit the sand.

With the blade in his hand, Joe marched to attack the Black Spirits who were draining the life out of Haley. As he neared, another tentacle burst through the hole, grabbed Joe by the knee and pulled him down. The blade flew out of his hand as he fell. Joe scrambled to find the blade as he fought off the tentacle. Able to get back up, Ryan spotted the blade, grabbed it, and lunged at the tentacle—severing its grasp on Joe. Ryan turned his attention to Haley, who was trying to scream out while being pulled toward the hole. Without hesitation, he grabbed the blade and ran toward Haley, yet quickly he realized he would not reach her in time—her body set to plunge into the hole.

"Good-bye, Ryan," she mouthed silently. Ryan yelled out to her. As he raced to Haley, an explosion was heard in the distance. Ryan looked back; it was Carl shouting and waving a lantern around. The noise and movement from Carl grabbed the attention of the Black Spirits, causing them to release Haley—tossing her aside. Carl ran in the opposite direction of the First Post, as the Black Spirits rushed towards him—moving in and out of the air.

After the Black Spirits had left, Ryan scurried to help an out-of-breath Haley. With assistance from Joe they bandaged her ankle and lifted her off the ground. As she thanked them, Ryan yelled to Joe, "What is Carl doing? They are going to kill him."

Joe stood up, picked up his bag and quietly spoke out to the group. "This is what he signed up for—to make sacrifices like this. It's time to go."

The entire group stared, enraptured, as Carl sprinting led a swarm of Black Spirits away from the group. "Carl has bought us time. We must keep quiet and move now," Joe reiterated to the group. In despair, they all grabbed their bags and walked hastily to the post. The only light allowing them to see ahead was the one provided by the blade Joe held in his hand.

As they moved silently on the cobblestone path, in the distance they could hear the Black Spirits crashing through Carl as he yelled out in agony.

CHAPTER 13

Ghost Town

"We're here," said Joe.

Ryan looked around, noticing a vastly different First Post from the one he had seen earlier. It was now completely dark, and the guards who had been at the entrance were no longer there. They passed the entrance, and all was quiet. The only sound came from the waterfall by the bridge where Ryan had seen Haley's family and the others go through.

"Where is everyone?" Tarien asked.

Armed with the blade, Joe walked over to one of the buildings and opened the door. No one was inside.

"What happened here?" Ryan asked Joe.

"I don't know," he replied.

As the group continued, a voice could be heard whispering near the benches. "Help! Help me please."

With the glow from the blade leading the way, the group followed Joe toward the voice. Nearing the benches, Joe moved the blade around to see where the voice was coming from. As he moved the light, a man lying on the ground came into view. Joe quickly walked over to the man, helped him sit up, and gave him water from his bag. Staring at the man, Ryan realized he was from the original group who had come to the post with him. Ryan went over and bent down next to the man.

"You are the one who didn't leave for the Realm. You weren't ready to leave, right?" Ryan asked the man.

The man nodded; cuts and bruises visible across the side of his face. "My name is Bill," the man said.

Interrupting the man, Haley asked, "What happened here? Where is everyone?"

"They are gone. All of them," Bill said, his voice tensing up as he began to recount what had transpired. "My wife, Sheryl, and I were in the building sitting down when we heard screaming coming from outside. One of the guards came into the room and told everyone to stay inside. That's when the alarm began to go off and the light went out. All of a sudden, inside the room, we saw something in the darkness—a pair of red, beaming eyes moving around the room, with a scowling noise. The creature began to attack as we all ran frantically, trying to find the door. I eventually was able find the door handle, and as I opened it, I was pelted over the head from behind. The next thing I knew, I woke up here by the benches and heard you guys."

Harry, listening from afar, shouted, "Sounds like a weak story to me, you being the only survivor! Why did they leave just you alive?"

"That's the question I keep asking myself," Bill replied.

Joe asked Ryan and Tarien to help Bill up from the ground and place him on the bench. As Ryan went to help, the whispering voice returned. "Ryan, we are coming for you. Join us."

Tensing up, Ryan said, "We have to get out of here! They are coming."

At that moment, the wind picked up around them. Joe quickly grabbed an extra bag that was nearby and gave it to Ryan. "This was one of the guard's. It will have resources for you to use against the Devamans. Take it with you," Joe said.

Unsure as to why Joe was handing him the bag, Ryan was about to speak up when an intense gust of wind rushed into the post. The force of the wind blew out all of the windows in the buildings. Everyone in the group dropped to the ground as glass shattered everywhere.

"Run, and follow the light from the bridge!" commanded Joe.

Ryan helped Cooper, his mother, and Haley up from the ground and told them to go. Tarien and James picked Bill up and headed off. Harry lay on the ground, pieces of glass stuck in his legs. Seeing Harry in pain, Joe went to help when a Black Spirit appeared and grabbed ahold of Harry and quickly vanished with him in its grasp. Shocked at this sight, Ryan swiftly placed the bag Joe gave him around his shoulders and raced toward the bridge. An obscure light by the bridge gave the group their heading.

As he neared the bridge, Ryan turned around to find Joe. In the distance Joe was seen with a blade in his hands surrounded by hundreds of Black Spirits.

"Ryan, we have to go!" said James.

As Ryan stared at the Black Spirits circling around Joe, he said with conviction, "I can't leave Joe. They are going to kill him."

Ryan grabbed the bag, and rummaged through until he found a blade. He threw the bag to Tarien and told them to go through the waterfall.

"Ryan, we are not going to leave without you," Haley said in despair.

"I have to help him," Ryan replied. He ran toward Joe.

As he neared Joe, the wind and shrieking sounds of the Devamans intensified. The Black Spirits disappeared and reappeared, swarming around him like vultures. Joe, with his blade lit up, swung it through the air with effectiveness as they neared.

"What are you doing?" Joe yelled, seeing Ryan. "You have to go now! I can't hold them off forever!"

Unfazed, Ryan shouted back, "You are not going to make it out. There are too many of them." As he finished his sentence, Ryan stood still as the Black Spirits began to converge together, taking the shape of an ogre-like creature. They came crashing in together, causing the creature to grow in size. The creature was black with visible red lumps across its body.

"Go now!" Joe shouted. Ryan remained motionless—until he noticed a Black Spirit rumbling through the ground toward him. "Go!" Joe yelled, spotting the Black Spirit. "I will be right behind you once I get rid of this thing."

With the Black Spirit charging toward him, Ryan began a sprint back to the bridge. He could hear Haley and Tarien yelling out to him. Ryan ran as fast as he could. Once on the bridge, he turned back ready to fight the Black Spirit—but when he turned it was not there. Instead he saw Joe battling the ogre. As Ryan caught his breath, he watched as Joe took a sweeping punch from the creature, knocking him down and tossing the blade from his hands. With Joe defenseless on the ground, two Black Spirits burst off of the creature—inching closer to finish off Joe.

"Joe, you have to get up!" Ryan shouted. Out of the corner of his eye, Ryan saw a figure in the distance dressed in a black trench coat with a hood. This new creature had fiery red eyes and black scaly skin with red streaks. As Ryan watched, he began to stumble down. A sharp pain shot through the right side of his chest. He felt the air rush out of him and gasped. All of the noise around him felt miles away. He heard the screams of Haley and the rest of the group. Trying to figure out what happened he raised his head to see a Black Spirit moving in and out of the air around him. Unable to stand, he reached for the blade but could not find it. As the Black Spirit came rushing to him, Ryan felt a bulge in his pocket and remembered the blue crystals Joe had given him. Ryan grabbed the bag and pulled out the crystals, and as the Black Spirit appeared in front of him, he tossed the crystals. While suspended in the air, the crystals exploded into illuminations, violently crashing into the Black Spirit.

Ryan felt all the energy draining out of his body. He began to see black spots. As he felt his consciousness fading away, someone grabbed him from behind and pulled him toward the waterfall. Just as he heard the sound of the water stop, all went dark.

CHAPTER 14

A Room of Memories

A month had passed since his father accident, and Ryan was in a dark place in his life. His mother asked him to go through his father's office in their house and decide which of his father's belongings he wanted to keep and which he did not. Ryan sat on the floor of his dad's office in a complete daze. He looked at his phone and saw twelve text messages had come in; he did not answer a single one. There was a voicemail from his coach; he didn't bother to listen. His phone vibrated as another text message came in. He was so sick and tired of everyone trying to check in on him and ask how he was feeling. He grabbed his phone, opened one of his father's desk drawers and shoved it in. He sat on his dad's desk chair, and as he sat there, he began to look around the office.

His father's office was exactly like his father—neat and organized. There was one long, mahogany desk with a glass top in the middle of the room. In front of the desk, there were two large bookcases, made from the same mahogany, against the wall. His desk was purely for business—he was an attorney. On the desk were his father's laptop which sat in the middle, a large desk calendar with notes and dates appointed offset to the right of the desk, a stapler and an assortment of pens placed neatly into a leather cup. There was a small two-drawer cabinet to the right of the desk with his printer placed atop of the cabinet.

When his dad was home, this is where he spent much of his time. Ryan knew he could not disturb his father when he was in his office. Ryan often overheard his dad preparing speeches for a conference, talking with his associate, Alex, until a case was settled, and many times, it was silent as if his father was not there at all.

While his father's desk was for business, the bookcases were filled with personal belongings and memories. It was a display of what a passionate man Ryan's father was. When facing the bookcases, the five-shelf bookcase to the left was filled with books. There were a handful of books just on the Titanic (his father always claimed he was on the Titanic in his past life because of his fear of cold water), books on different events in history—the Civil War, the World Wars, Pearl Harbor—books on the universe, and so on. His eclectic taste could be seen throughout the shelves of this bookcase. The bookcase to the right was filled with memories of his father's life. On the two bottom shelves there was a flag from a sleepaway camp his father went to when he was just a boy, a sweater neatly folded with the embroidery from his fraternity stitched onto it and one trophy he won from a track-and-field competition (his father always bragged about it). On the top of the two bookcases were many of Ryan's trophies. "Athlete of the Year," "Most Valuable Player," and "Best Hitter," were just a few of the accomplishments engraved on the trophies. On the three top shelves, there were at least fifteen picture frames.

Ryan picked himself up from the chair and began to look at the bookcases. Memories were all he saw. He glanced at all the pictures of him with his dad. He couldn't fathom deciding which belongings to keep or throw away. He was crushed by the finality of getting rid of his father's things. How could he never see him again? How could he never play catch with his father again? How would he not be able to hear his voice yelling from the stands during one of his games? Who was going to give him advice on all of life's obstacles?

How could he ever tell his dad again how much he loved him? What hurt the most were the opportunities he had missed to spend extra time with his father.

He began to cry as he sifted through the pictures of him and his father: the first baseball game they went to, all of the football games, Ryan's amazing all-star catch in the outfield to win the game, and the two of them sitting together, watching their favorite television show. Someone's entire life was now a room of memories. With tears rolling down, Ryan continued to sift through his father's belongings, when a piece of paper caught Ryan's attention. He opened the paper that was neatly folded into a perfect square and saw its title: "The Father I Hope to Be." Underneath the title, the following was written: "I hope to be a father who teaches his son to always do what is right, to be honest, to be a gentleman, to be a man of faith, and to always stand up for those who are less fortunate than we are. Lastly, I hope to be a father who teaches his son to laugh, to be happy, to have friends and to love his family." As he finished reading, Ryan grabbed his phone and threw it against the wall. "What am I supposed to do now, Dad?!" he shouted. "Where do I go from here?"

"Open your eyes, Ryan. Open your eyes." Ryan looked around the room, but saw no one. "Ryan, you need to wake up. We need to keep moving," the voice in the distance said. He heard the command, but he did not want to move. He did not want to leave his father's office. So he sat down in his father's favorite chair and closed his eyes as hard as he could; wishing the voices away.

CHAPTER 15

The Forest

When Ryan opened his eyes, light entered from his new surroundings.

"Guys, come here. He woke up!" Haley said excitedly.

Lying on the floor, he saw Tarien and James come over—smiles on their faces. "I don't know how you made it, but man, it's great to see you back," James said as he extended his arm out to him. Ryan grabbed his arm and tried to pull himself up, but a sharp pain in his right chest would not let him. He asked what had happened.

"You don't remember?" Haley asked.

"You took one of those spirits right through the chest," Tarien blurted out. "I don't know how you survived."

Feeling the pain, he lifted up his shirt and a round black mark was etched into his chest. When he touched it, pain permeated throughout his body.

"What about Joe? Is he here?" Ryan asked.

The three of them looked at each other, and Haley said, "Ryan, he never made it through."

Ryan put his head down between his knees. He could feel the anger, frustration, and sadness all at once. He took a deep breath. "What are we going to do now? Who will protect us?"

"We'll figure it out," Haley said as she put her hand on his shoulder.

"Let's just follow the new path and hope we have a safe passage," James said as he pointed to a perfectly paved brown-sand path.

As they helped Ryan to his feet, he took a moment to look at his surroundings. It was a beautiful forest filled with light and the most rare trees and flowers he had ever seen. The path ahead was made up of green plants—diminutive in size—with bright blue flowers flowing out. These plants went on for miles on both sides of the path. In between the green plants were trees whose outer bark went up roughly eighteen feet. Attached to the bark were branches with green leaves which appeared somewhat florescent. What was unusual was they were not outside, but in a cave-like dome with a rocky ceiling hundreds of miles up. Behind him, was the tunnel from which they had come.

"Where are we now?" Ryan asked in amazement. No one knew the answer. As they continued to look around, Cooper and his mom showed up on the path—Cooper ran and gave Ryan a hug. Ryan grimaced in pain.

"Well, it's about time," said a voice to the right of Ryan. It was Bill, who appeared out of the trees to his right. "Let's stop lying around," he said.

"Are we safe from the Black Spirits?" Ryan asked as he snapped out of his daze. "Why aren't there any guards around to guide us?"

Once again, no one knew the answer. James grabbed his bag, put it on, and said, "I don't know, but let's start moving."

The seven of them began to walk through the brown-sand path. There were hundreds of different species of birds flying around or perched on the trees. Each of the birds was just as colorful as the flowers and trees around them. As birds flew overhead, the scenery of the path ahead of the group began to change.

The trees now in front of the group were packed with striking yellow leaves. The trees on both sides of the path connected above them, sending down a continuous flow of bright yellow leaves onto the path—like snow falling. The aroma of the forest was fresh and smelled of flowers. Cooper, walking ahead of the group, turned back to his mom and said, "If this is what is before the Realm, imagine how magical the Realm must be."

As they walked, Ryan talked with Tarien and James and learned that they had much in common. Tarien and James were childhood friends who both played baseball.

"So what led you to the Realm?" Ryan asked.

They explained that they had recently graduated from high school; however, their parents had lost their jobs at a steel plant and could not afford to send them to college. The two of them were desperate to go to college and have a chance to play baseball. They began to work double shifts at a local restaurant to make money to pay for school. One day, a man named Walter, dressed in a nice navy-blue suit told them of a place where they could play baseball and go to school for free. The two of them thought it had to have been a hoax and did not believe the man. It wasn't until the fourth or fifth time he showed up that they finally sat down with him and went over all of the pamphlets—they were sold.

Strolling through the raining yellow leaves, Ryan heard a noise he had not heard before. He gazed around but spotted only the leaves careening down. Thinking it was in his mind he continued forward.

CHAPTER 16

Spies in the Sky

As the group continued, a loud squawking sound was heard in the distance. It was high in pitch causing the group to stop moving—each of them covering their ears. The noise did not belong as it disturbed the calmness and serenity of the forest.

"That does not sound good," Haley said nervously. Afraid the Black Spirits had returned, the group picked up their pace. The squawking persisted and grew louder. The group walked quickly as they left the yellow leave path and found themselves in a lush multi-colored rain forest. With massive trees and flowers all around both sides of the path, the beauty was once again awe-inspiring. Entering this area, Ryan stopped to gaze behind him, as he did his eyes spotted two immense black vultures. In shock Ryan mumbled a couple of words, as the rest of the group turned around and spotted what Ryan did—human-sized vultures. These creatures were scaly and bony as if they had not consumed food in ages. As the vultures spotted the group, they began to fly towards them.

"Okay, something tells me these birds are not friendly," James said.

"Into the forest!" Tarien shouted.

"Ryan, do you care if you live or die?"

Ryan was sitting on a couch inside of a psychologist's office looking out of the window.

"Well, do you?" a middle-aged man asked as he sat in a chair about seven feet away from Ryan, who continued to ignore him. "We still have another forty-five minutes, so I can keep asking questions until you answer," the man said.

Annoyed with the questions and his surroundings, Ryan inhaled, sighed, and said, "Dr. Ronaldo, it was not my choice to come here. My mom hounded me to come, so if you don't mind, I would like to sit here in silence for the next forty-five minutes."

The man jotted notes down on a notepad and placed it on the desk next to him. "So do you care or not?"

Angry, Ryan shouted back, "What does it matter? We all die anyway. So who cares what I think. Eventually time runs out on everyone."

The man stared at an irritated Ryan and said, "Just because we all are going to die, does not mean we can't enjoy the time we have."

Weaving in out of the branches and bushes, Ryan yelled out, as he could not spot anyone from the group. As the vultures circled above the forest searching for their prey, Ryan stopped running, turned around, and whispered, "Where are you guys?" No one responded. He tensed up at the thought of being alone.

"Ryan, what are you scared of?" Dr. Ronaldo asked.

Holding back the tears that were building behind his eyes, Ryan looked away from the doctor as he tried to compose himself. Eventually, he faced the doctor and said, "I am afraid of living in a world without him. I have lost the person who guided me my whole life and taught me how to be a man. I am afraid that I will fail in living up to the man he would want me to be. I am afraid to move on without him by my side. I am afraid to have fun, and I am especially afraid that one day, as the years go by, he will become a distant memory. I don't want my memories of him to fade away. And that is what I am afraid of."

Everything was spinning. Ryan leaned against a tree, sweating, until he felt a soft hand on his shoulder.

"Ryan, are you okay?"

Ryan turned around and saw the face that had kept him going on this journey. "Haley, where were you? Where is everyone?" he asked.

With a look of exhaustion, she replied, "I don't know. In all the confusion, I just lost all sense of direction and wound up alone. I am so glad I found you."

Ryan was able to regain his composure. "I think we need to head back to the path and hope that the rest of the group does the same."

Suddenly, out of one of the bushes to their left, Tarien appeared, startling them both.

"Tarien, where is everyone?" they asked. But he did not know either. They told Tarien their plan to go back to the path, and he agreed. As they walked, Haley and Tarien, both with their bags around their shoulders, looked up as the shrieking noise from the vultures reverberated through the forest trees.

"Why do I only see one?" Tarien asked.

"One what?" Haley responded.

And with that, the three of them heard a thud several yards away, causing the birds in the forest to flee.

"That can't be good!" Ryan whispered out.

The three of them quickly hid behind a tree.

"Should we run?" Haley whispered.

"If we run, it will hear us. Let's just stay here and wait until it goes away," Tarien whispered back.

Ryan poked his head out from behind the tree. Ahead, through creases between the branches, he saw the vulture walking and moving its head from side to side in search of them. The three stood still for nearly five minutes as the noise from the vulture grew louder and louder—and then a second violent thud came from their left— the other vulture.

Knowing they had to act fast, Ryan shouted out to run. The vulture to the left crashed through the branches and trees and stood directly in front of them—they remained motionless. They stood in horror as the vulture stared straight in their direction.

"At the count of three, we go," whispered Tarien. "One … two …"

Before he could say three, James appeared from the branches to their right and yelled out, "There you guys are! I have been looking for you everywhere. What are you doing?"

"Look ahead," whispered Tarien.

Confused, James spotted the vulture and turned white as a ghost as he stared at the bone-and-flesh vulture in front of him.

At that moment the other vulture crashed through trees and violently took James down with its claws, pierced his right thigh and began to pick him up. Tarien, without hesitation, ran to James's aid and pried him away from the vulture. As the vulture was about to strike Tarien, Ryan rushed in and sliced through one of its legs with a blade found in the bag Joe had given him. The noise from the wounded vulture was deafening. At the sight of the blade, the second vulture took flight.

Tarien and Ryan pulled James to his feet as he writhed in pain. James put his arms around them. "Let's go!" yelled Ryan. Haley led the charge forward as Tarien and Ryan dragged James. There was another loud cry. Ryan looked back and saw the injured vulture shake violently in pain. Smoke began to flow down from the vulture towards the ground, as the vulture disintegrated. The smoke began to move in circular motion and hissing sounds could be heard from inside. As the smoke cleared, visible to them were hundreds of black and red snakes slithering toward them, and growing in size as they did.

"Ryan, what are the regrets you have about your father?" Dr. Ronaldo asked. Ryan began to pull his keys out of his pocket after noticing that the session was coming to an end.

"Regrets?" Ryan replied. "Doc, people always have regrets when looking back at the past, but when you lose someone, regrets are harder to let to go. My biggest regret is that I wasn't able to tell my father, one last time, how much I loved him and how much he meant to me. He was my hero, and I wish I had been the type of son who, whenever his dad asked for help, would have done it without hesitation. But the older I got, the more stubborn and difficult I became."

Ryan stood up as the hour-long session finally drew to a close. The doctor, noticing the rush Ryan was in, asked him, "Do you feel this session helped? Do you feel that you're able to let go some of the weight you have been carrying? Because everyone is concerned. They are worried that you have completely given up on school, baseball, family and friends. Staying home every day playing your regrets over and over again in your head is not a life. I know it's hard to hear this now, but time will heal all wounds."

Not listening to the doctor, Ryan walked toward the door. As he opened it, he looked back and said, "I appreciate your concern, but you know how people say tomorrow is another day? Well, it is absolutely true, but when that sun rises tomorrow my father will still be gone, and nothing will change that."

"James, hold on. Keep your eyes open," shouted Haley as Ryan and Tarien carried his frail body forward. The noise of the snakes slithering behind them grew more intense, but they could not move fast enough under the weight of James's body.

"We are not going to make it," Tarien shouted.

They pushed through the forest, knocking down branch after branch.

"I see a light!" Haley said, pointing to a spot in the distance. As they neared the light, Haley shouted, "It's a cabin!"

With the hope of survival, the boys urged James on as they moved swiftly. They pressed through a bulky group of branches, and then there it was—a cabin in the middle of nowhere. At that moment, Ryan gazed back, and the snakes were gone.

CHAPTER 17

The Cabin

The cabin was of moderate size and made of beautiful mahogany wood; much like the wood of his father's desk. A light was on inside the cabin, and smoke was coming out of the chimney. As they neared the cabin, they saw a hefty sized rock to their right with the engraving "*Nolite Timere.*"

"Where did the snakes go?" Ryan said as an explosion was heard in the distance, causing the lighting inside the forest to dim ever so slightly. The four of them stopped in front of the cabin.

"Ryan, your pocket," Haley said.

Ryan looked down at his pocket which was glowing. He had forgotten about it. He pulled out the key and showed it to them. Tarien and Haley had questions about the Key, but they knew James had to get aid immediately. They trudged forward, inching closer to the porch that wrapped around the cabin.

"I wonder who is inside the house," Haley said.

"We can't worry about that right now. We have to get inside and get James help," Tarien replied. James, his shirt soaked in blood, was battling to keep his eyes open. As they neared the steps of the porch, a man was heard humming. The noise was coming from the right side of the porch.

"That is a creepy," whispered Haley.

Ryan, listening intently to the man's voice, stopped walking. "I know that song."

"Champ, what's wrong?" Ryan's dad asked as he sat on his bed.

Eight-year-old Ryan sat up. "I can't fall asleep. When I close my eyes, my mind thinks too much."

"Champ, I have the same problem with my mind. It is always working and trying to dump stuff in my head, but you know what I do? I just brush it aside. Don't let your conscience get the best of you."

His father's words comforted him and Ryan asked, "How did you fall asleep when you were a young boy?"

"I would put the radio on and listened to some music," his father replied.

"Can you sing me a song?" Ryan asked, as he closed his eyes.

Ryan's father agreed and sang:

> I'll be there to guide you through the night.
> I will follow with a shining light.
> Don't be afraid to be alone,
> 'Cause I will lead you home.
> So don't be afraid, my son—
> The morning will bring the sun.
> Whenever doubt creeps into your mind,
> My love and my hand you will always find.
> So just dream, dream away.
> Wherever you go, it will be okay.
> So stand and be strong, my son.
> Tomorrow brings the sun.

"What do you mean you know that song?" Tarien asked.

"My father sang it to me when I was a kid," Ryan said as he moved across the porch toward the sound. When he reached the right side of the porch, in front of him stood a rocking chair with its back to Ryan. A gentleman was sitting in the chair, and upon hearing Ryan's footsteps, ceased humming. A million thoughts raced through Ryan's head as the man stood up. Who was he? How could he know that song? Why was he in this place?

CHAPTER 18

Emily, Landry, and Ian

The man stood up and turned to face Ryan. He was in his late forties; about five-foot nine, medium build with thinning brown hair. He was dressed in khaki pants and a buttoned down blue shirt. As he stared at Ryan, he moved away from the rocking chair, which was at a dominoes table with an additional chair on the other side. He stared at Ryan for a couple of seconds and smiled. "It's good to see you, Ryan."

Surprised the man knew his name, Ryan moved aside to show the injuries James had sustained. He asked the man if they could use the cabin to attend to James wounds.

"Of course," the man said before leading them inside the cabin through the back entrance. As they entered, Ryan noticed the cabin was decorated in an early 1900's fashion and was extremely well kept and clean. They passed through the kitchen and went into the living room, where they laid James down on a couch.

"Emily!" the man shouted. "Emily, please bring the first aid kit. Our guests have arrived."

Haley looked over at Ryan, confused. As she opened her mouth to ask the gentleman a question, a woman in her late forties, small in stature, with short brown hair entered the room. She was holding a white first aid kit in her hand.

She handed the kit to the gentleman before turning to Ryan. "You must be Ryan. It's great to see you."

She walked over to help disinfect James's wounds and place bandages around them. "He will be all right. He just needs to get some sleep, and he should heal just fine," she said to them. She then motioned Haley, Tarien, and Ryan to the kitchen, where she made them some tea.

Emily was a sweet woman who showed true interest in learning how they ended up in the forest. The three of them were thrilled to be sitting down, unafraid of being attacked. After they talked for nearly an hour, the gentleman entered the room, followed by another man. This man must have been in his late forties as well, was about six feet tall and lean. He had a round face with thick black hair. He was dressed in a pair of jeans and a short-sleeved button-down shirt with dirt on it. He looked disheveled as if he had been gardening all day.

"I have secured our surroundings. We should be safe here for a day or two, but with the light in the forest now dimming, we cannot stay here for any amount of time longer than that," the man said to Emily and the other gentleman. Then he turned to Ryan. With a huge smile on his face, he walked over to him and held out his hand. Ryan was yet again caught off guard by the attention he was receiving from these unknown hosts. He hesitantly shook the man's hand.

"It is good to see you," the man said. "My name is Ian. This fine gentleman to my right is my best friend, Landry and this is his wife Emily. We have been waiting for your arrival and are glad to help you all get to the Realm. I know you must have so many questions, but I'm sure you are exhausted and could use some rest. You will need it to continue the journey."

Before Ryan could say anything, Emily spoke up and requested they follow her to a large guest room where three beds were prepared.

The room was pristine and perfectly maintained. On the walls were several framed pictures of individuals. Emily grabbed Tarien's and Haley's bags and put them in the closet before asking if they needed anything else.

"Emily, thank you for your hospitality and for helping James, but we have so many questions," Ryan said.

"There will be time for all of that after you rest. The end of this journey will not be an easy one, and you will need your strength," she said. She walked out of the room leaving Ryan more confused than ever.

CHAPTER 19

All Is Lost

"Ryan, it's time for you to say a few words," his uncle leaned over and whispered.

Ryan, dressed in a black suit, stood up. His mom gave him a kiss as he passed her and left the row. He walked passed the casket, placed his right hand on top of it and moved to the altar of the church. With each step he took, the pain and fury grew inside him. He reached the podium, placed the microphone in front of him and looked out at the substantial number of family members and friends in attendance. They were all waiting for him to put his father's fifty years of life into a five-minute speech. Ryan pulled out a piece of paper from his suit pocket, unfolded it and began to read it out loud.

"My father ... my father was a great man. He ..." At that moment, Ryan's eyes began to fill with tears, and the anger inside of him boiled. He looked away from the paper and spoke.

"Life is brutal. I learned this just two days ago. It doesn't matter how good of a person you are or how kind you are. My father was both of these and more but apparently God needed him more than his family did. So live while you have the chance."

With that, he walked away from the podium and down the aisle. He did not stop until he was out of the church. Standing outside he felt as if he was suffocating. Ryan loosened his tie and as he did the whispering voice returned: "Ryan, the end is near. A time will soon come when you have to decide if you want to join the right side. No more pain. Join us and it all goes away."

The voice vanished and Ryan's eyes opened. He was sweating as he scanned the room and realized he was lying down in a bed in the cabin.

Unable to go back to sleep, Ryan stood up and began to walk out of the room. Reaching the door, he turned back and saw Haley and Tarien sleeping. Both seemed restless, as if in a nightmare. As Ryan moved toward Haley to wake her up, he heard voices whispering outside the room. His curiosity getting the best of him, he gently opened the door as quietly as he could and walked until he reached the end of the hallway which connected to the living room.

He poked his head out to see who was speaking. He saw James lying on the couch in the same restless sleep as Haley and Tarien. Several feet from the couch were Ian and Landry sitting at the dining room table.

Determined to find out what was going on, Ryan eavesdropped on the conversation.

"The light is beginning to fade, and what we feared is coming to pass. It doesn't look like Joe made it out, so we are going to have to move on without him," Ian announced.

Landry jumped in and stated, "With each passing moment, the Devamans grow stronger. They now have more power and ability to defeat us, and Ryan has yet to learn his true potential."

As Ryan tried to move closer, he stumbled upon a desk next to the hallway. Landry and Ian discontinued their conversation. Ryan hastily tiptoed back to the guest room. As he opened the door, he heard Haley. "Ryan, what are you doing?"

Ryan looked over and Haley was sitting up in her bed. Ryan strolled over to her, as Tarien was sleeping soundly, and sat down on the bed. He explained to her what he had just heard from Ian and Landry.

"What does all this mean? And why do they know so much about you?" Haley whispered.

Ryan shrugged. "I don't know."

"Why are you always so serious, Ryan? I have yet to see you smile or laugh," she asked. "When was the last time you did?"

At that moment, Ryan let down the wall he had put up between him and the rest of the world, and said, "The last time I truly laughed was probably about four months ago, when I saw my father try to parallel park between two cars. He played bumper cars as he tried to fit in." Thinking of that moment, Ryan smiled. "The best part about it was that when my mother and I tried to explain to him what had just happened, he had no idea he had done it. He was oblivious."

Haley laughed with him. "So what went so wrong? Why are you carrying such pain?"

Seeing how much Haley cared, he confided in her. He spoke of the past months, his father's passing and all the emotions that came with it. For the first time in a long time, Ryan felt truly connected to someone and he did not want it to go away.

Ryan finished his story as Haley held his hand. In that moment, Ryan felt his heart racing. He felt something with Haley he had never felt before. He took one of his hands and placed it on Haley's hip. As he leaned in to kiss her, Landry entered the room shouting.

"Someone is outside! Someone is coming toward the cabin!"

CHAPTER 20

Who Is Coming?

Haley and Ryan sprung off the bed, while Tarien woke up in state of confusion. They quickly followed Landry out of the room. Haley and Tarien continued down the hallway, as Landry grabbed Ryan by the arm and said, "Son, I know you are all confused, but one thing you can't do is fall for that one," pointing at Haley.

Ryan shrugged it off and walked toward the living room area. As he made his way into the room, James remained sleeping and Emily and Ian were staring out the window.

"Who is coming?" Haley asked.

"They have to be human. The perimeters set up would have sent out flashing lights if it were the Devamans," Landry proclaimed.

Haley peeked through the window.

"Haley, what is it?" Ryan asked, as she dashed toward the front door.

As she opened the door, she yelled, "It's my brothers!"

Eric and Dan, bruised and scraped all over their bodies, walked with heavy feet toward the stairs of the front porch. Haley ran to her brothers and gave them both a hug. Following close behind them was Bill. His appearance was similar to theirs as he trudged forward. Standing outside, Ryan took note of how the light in the forest had dimmed since they had first arrived. He thought of what Ian and Landry had said of running out of time. With the light fading, the fear of the return of the Black Spirits crept into Ryan's mind.

He looked over at Landry and Ian, who were pointing toward the horizon, mapping out a route to the Second Post. As Haley continued to speak with her brothers, Tarien and James appeared on the porch. "What is all this commotion about?" a suddenly spry James said.

Emily came outside to help the three newly arrived guests into the house.

"What happened out there?" Haley asked with excitement.

As they all walked inside the cabin, Landry and Ian stayed behind and called Ryan over to them. Ryan, who had been following Haley into the cabin, stopped, turned around, and looked over at the two gentlemen. As Haley stared at Ryan, he motioned to her to go ahead inside without him. "There are things I need to find out." He walked toward the porch steps where the two men sat.

"Ryan, we don't have much time left. The light is fading, and soon we will have to move through the forest in the dark with the enemy near," Ian said.

Ryan tired of the continued vague responses, replied, "Much time left for what?!"

"Joe was supposed to have shown you who you are," Landry added. "You are not like the rest of us. You are a Keeper."

"A keeper of what? What does that mean?" Ryan asked.

The two gentlemen looked at each other, and Landry responded, "Ryan, you are the Keeper of the Peace. That Key you have in your pocket was given to you for a reason. You are meant to help keep the dark forces away with the powers inside of you."

Ryan rolled his eyes and began to step away from the two men and head back to the cabin.

"Ryan," Ian called, "you have to learn to have faith, to love, to believe, and to let all of the anger you have inside drift away. You were once so carefree. You were once so happy. You are now at a breaking point where you have two different paths to choose from. Where are you headed, Ryan Shepard?"

Ryan's eyes opened wide and the rage inside spewed out. "Who in the world are you guys? How do you know anything about me? It is absurd that I have superhero powers that will save everyone in your precious Realm, which, by the way, sounds like it doesn't exist. Everyone here has probably been sold a bunch of garbage. I am tired of all the cryptic messages and bizarre events. I don't care about this place. There is nothing here for me. I am only here right now because of a promise I had made to Haley. Thank you for letting us use your place, but it's time for me to go."

Finishing his rant, he turned his back to the two men and walked back to the cabin.

"Ryan, we are sorry you feel this way," Landry replied. "The truth is that we share a similar connection. We all have lost someone we love, but the way we honor those we have lost is in the way we live on after them. I knew your father, and he would have wanted you to live and let go."

Ryan stopped walking. "How did you know my father?"

Ian looked at Landry and said, "Like we said, our paths are connected. Your father was an amazing man, a true gentleman who loved his life, loved his family, and absolutely adored you."

Having heard enough, Ryan turned around and headed inside. As he inched closer to the porch steps, he said, "If you knew my father, you would know that he was taken, way before his time."

Fuming as he entered the cabin, he saw everyone gathered around Eric, Dan, and Bill as they continued their story of how they had ended up at the cabin. His mind made up, Ryan began to make his way around everyone and toward the hallway. From the corner of his eye, he saw Haley turn her head to look at him—he avoided making eye contact with her and marched on without hesitation. He went into the room and grabbed the bag Joe had given him. Haley walked in. Ryan looked at her and saw the confused look on her face. He felt sorry for what he was about to do, but Landry and Ian speaking of his father was the last straw. He was done with this place.

"What are you doing, Ryan? Where are you going?" she asked.

Ryan put his head down in shame and looked back up. "Haley, you have your brothers back, and I am so happy for you. But you don't need me anymore to help find Dylan or to get to the Realm. It's time for me to go back home."

Haley stood in front of the door. "What about everybody telling you that you are special? You are someone everyone believes in—but you have no faith in yourself."

Ryan looked into Haley's eyes and said, "I am no one. I am just another person. We are all just a blip in time, and my leaving here will make no difference. All those around me seem to vanish—my dad, for one, and now Joe. You are all better off without me. I wish you the best of luck, Haley."

As he moved forward, she stepped aside, but before he passed, she grabbed his arm. "Ryan Shepard, I hope you find whatever it is you are looking for."

Ryan made his way down the hallway and passed the rest of the group. Unwilling to go through more good-byes, he said nothing as he went to the front door. When he opened the door, the light outside had grown dimmer. Landry and Emily were in the yard, preparing bags for their trek to the Second Post. When they saw Ryan, they stopped packing and walked over to him.

"Are you sure you don't want to come with us, Ryan?" Emily asked.

Once she realized there was no dissuading him, she lunged forward to give him a hug. Landry came over and shook Ryan's hand and told him how to find his way to the brown-sand path and back to the First Post. Ian handed Ryan a small bag with weapons and supplies in case he ran into any problems. Ryan peeked inside the bag—a new blade and a container of blue crystals. Ian reached into his pocket and handed Ryan a small gold ball. "When it gets too dark, push down on the button on top of the ball, and it will give you the light you need." He shook Ryan's hand. "I wish you nothing but the best and hope one day our paths cross again," Ian said.

After the good-byes Ryan made his way toward the forest. Before entering, he looked back at the cabin and saw Haley staring out at him through one of the windows. He turned back around and ignored the pain he felt in the pit of his stomach.

CHAPTER 21

All Alone

With darkness on the horizon, Ryan made his way through the forest, following the path Landry had lain out. As he walked, his decision to leave Haley tormented him. He pushed branches aside, keeping an eye out for the Devamans and any other unwelcome creatures. As he continued, he realized he was going in circles. He was seeing the same trees, branches, and flowers repeatedly. As time passed, the darkness settled further into the forest, and voices emerged in the air. He feared that he had made the wrong choice in leaving the group. He began to sweat as the thought of the dark engulfing him crept in his mind. What kept him moving was a phrase his father used to tell him at night when he had trouble sleeping: "Champ do not fear darkness, because where it exists, light always follows."

As the dark crept all around, Ryan remembered the gold ball Ian had given him. He dove into his pocket and took it out. Looking at the shiny round ball, Ryan noticed numeric symbols all around. As unknown noises in the forest emerged and nightfall surrounded him, he pressed the button on top of the ball. The ball began to shake as it lay in the palm of his hand. It rose into the air and expanded slightly in size. Floating in the air, the ball spun rapidly, spewing out a bright light that lit up the area around Ryan by ten feet. The ball did not move until Ryan moved forward; as he did, the ball moved in sync with him. The light allowed Ryan to see and he walked forward, hoping to find his way home.

Ryan was able to make his way through the forest and eventually found the brown-sand path. He was relieved to be on his way back home. By the light of the golden ball, he took step after step, following the path back to the First Post. He could almost feel himself lying down in his own bed again. The relief he felt was short-lived, as a gust of wind blew through the forest and the whispering voice returned.

"Ryan, I am here. What is there for you back home but sadness and anger? Come with me."

Ryan looked ahead and a shadowy figure standing at the right side of the path became visible. The figure stood about eight feet tall, but Ryan could not make out what or who it was. He stood still and yelled out, "Who is there? I am just trying to pass through and get back home."

The figure did not move. Ryan moved forward ever so slightly, allowing the light from the ball to illuminate the path ahead. With each step he took closer to the figure, he could feel his heart racing. He reached inside his bag and grabbed the blue crystals. "Listen, I don't want any problems." The light inched closer, revealing a portion of the shadowy figure. Its feet were dark black, with streams of fire inside. Ryan realized it was the same figure he had seen in the distance when Joe was warding off the Black Spirits at the First Post.

Fearful that this might be the Dark Shadow, he stopped in his tracks and began to step back. Two fire-laced eyes opened from the shadowy figure, and the whispering voice returned.

"Now is the time, Ryan. You can live a life that you can control. No sorrow. No pain."

The shadowy figure made its first move, opening its hand to reveal a square red object.

"I don't want any trouble. Just let me pass through," Ryan pleaded, continuing to backpedal as the figure moved closer. Ryan stopped his movement and shouted, "I warned you to let me be!"

He tossed the blue crystals toward the figure. As the crystals were suspended in the air, they exploded, shooting light from all directions at the figure. The lights rocketing to the creature, it raised its hands and created a dark circular liquid force field around it to deflect the light. Surprised the crystals did not affect the creature, Ryan raced in the opposite direction. As he ran, he looked back—the figure hadn't moved. Instead it heaved the square object in its hand at Ryan. As the object hit the ground, it rolled toward him. Ryan turned left, dashing into the forest. The object stopped moving and began to change shape. It opened up, and legs appeared. As Ryan looked back, the object reached its final form—a black spider expanding in size.

Ryan continued to run as he entered the heart of the forest. Not knowing where the creature was he looked around his surroundings, until he heard the trees behind him tumble to the ground, as the Spider barreled through any object in its path. Ryan ran once again and as he did his left foot became intertwined in some vines and shrubs—he fell to the ground. He tried to pull his leg out from the vines' grasp, but did not succeed. The trees ahead continued to tumble closer to Ryan as he lay on the forest ground.

Ryan feared the worse when all became silent. The silence lasted a minute. Suddenly, a high pitched screech broke the calm. Ryan looked around trying to determine where the sound was coming from. He spotted it about fifty feet away—a spider nearly his same height. Ryan felt a sense of hope when the spider, due to its increased size, could not make it past two enormous trees separating them. As Ryan attempted to get his foot out of the vines, he looked back and saw the spider shaking uncontrollably. Moments later, it disintegrated into black smoke drifting down towards the ground. Once the smoke evaporated, hundreds of miniature red and black spiders were seen making their way toward Ryan as he desperately attempted to get his foot out of the grip of the vines. "Come on!" he shouted as the swarm of spiders made their way to him. He was able to finally get his leg free and run again. As he did, he felt a pain and discomfort in his back. His body began to feel numb, and his movements became erratic and slow. He looked behind him—four spiders were on his shoulder and arms. His eyesight became fuzzy, as he stumbled forward. Then, a thundering light blew through the forest, knocking him down and fading everything to black.

CHAPTER 22

The Return

Still in his suit from the funeral, Ryan entered his room and slammed the door. Looking around, he became enraged at the sight of past memories—pictures, frames, and trophies. He began tossing any object he could grab against the walls. He took a framed picture of him and his parents on a ski vacation and flung it—glass shattered on the floor. All of his notebooks and school papers on his desk were whipped to the ground with one thunderous swoop. The rage continued for several more minutes until Ryan felt completely exhausted. With nothing left in his path to throw he collapsed to the floor in pain.

Completely broken inside, angry at the world and at God, he sat by his bed and put his face in his hands. He knew life would not stop because he had lost his father, but he wanted it to. Tomorrow, the sun would rise, and a new day would begin for everyone else, while he was left to deal with this anguish on his own. He knew that the baseball coach would give him a week or two to grieve and then want him back on the field. He knew his friends would be there for him at all times in the first few weeks but would eventually go back to consuming their life fretting over petty matters. How would he ever go back to normalcy?

Sitting on the floor, he picked his head up and stared at a picture that had not been destroyed during his rage. It was of him and his dad at a college football game. They had taken a road trip to see their favorite team. The game started off as a blowout with their team down by as many as twenty-one points. Ryan became distraught at the thought of their team losing, but his father kept telling him not lose hope. "Champ, as long as there is time on the clock, they have a chance." The picture had been taken after their team's miraculous comeback, and a young Ryan and his dad were smiling from ear to ear. Gazing at the picture, Ryan kept muttering the words his father had repeated throughout the game: "Don't lose hope. Don't lose hope."

Ryan's eyes opened, and he was staring up into the dark abyss of the forest. His body was numb and tingling. He attempted to move his arms and legs but was unable. He was only capable of mustering up enough strength to move his head. To his right, was the gloom of the forest, and to his left, a fire was lit under a dozen twigs. His mind began to wonder who could have possibly built that fire. As different scenarios played out in his head, he attempted to call out for help. All he could do was mumble. Frantically, he tried to sit up but did not have enough sensation in his body to do so. As he stared at the fire, a small black pot was seen on the ground with a bag beside it.

"Who is there?" he was finally able to say.

Ryan heard a noise from behind him—someone was walking through the forest, making their way toward him. Sensing the worst, Ryan tried as hard possible to somehow get his body to respond to his mind's request to move, but nothing happened. The noise got closer and closer until it finally stopped right behind Ryan. Fearing the end, he closed his eyes for a second, and when he reopened them, he saw a face he did not expect.

"Did you miss me?!" Joe said, smirking. "Don't waste too much energy. The poison from the spiders is still in your system, but I made you a remedy that should help speed up the recovery process." Joe went over to the pot and placed a silver flask inside it. He walked back to Ryan, lifted his head, and poured the liquid into his mouth. Joe informed him that inside the flask were minerals and herbal spices from the forest. Around five minutes later, Ryan was able to regain sensation in his body and finally able to stand up.

Trying to wrap his head around the idea of Joe being back, Ryan asked, "Joe, how did you make it out?"

Joe picked up his bag and put it around his shoulders before handing Ryan his own. "There isn't time to get into specifics, as there is a traitor amongst us. Everyone you have met or have been in contact with could be operating with the Devamans."

Ryan could not possibly imagine anyone from his group betraying them.

"Ryan, what were you doing out here all alone? Why aren't you with the rest of the group?" Joe asked.

The question hurt Ryan, as he now thought of Haley being in danger. "I just wanted to go home, but if Haley is in trouble, I am coming with you," Ryan replied.

Joe with a blade in his hand used its glow to guide the two through the forest. As they moved, Joe told Ryan of a survivor he met in the First Post who had communicated to him that someone from the inside was helping sabotage the Blue Alley, allowing the Devamans to make their way toward the Realm with the least amount of resistance as possible.

"Someone has been messing with the lights in the Blue Alley and tipping off the Devamans about you and your group's location," Joe explained as they walked. "This means that the group you left is going to be ambushed, and my guess is that it will be at the Second Post. And you need to know that as the Black Spirits continue to move closer to the Realm, they grow in strength and their human features become more prevalent. The lack of guards around to guide can only signify that a battle is upon us.

Ryan turned to Joe and asked if he had ever waged a war like this with the Devamans.

"I was not part of the last attempt to seize the Realm. As at that time, I didn't even know about this place. But from what I have been told, it was a war that finished with much suffering. In the end, though, the Keeper who was brought in was able to close off the Realm right before evil could enter," Joe responded.

Ryan proceeded to inquire about Landry, Ian, and Emily and all the points they had mentioned back at the cabin.

"They are good people. They each asked to come on their own from the Realm to make sure that you succeed on your journey. And in regards to you having something special inside, that is all true. Here, you are different from everyone else, but until you learn to believe in yourself and let go of the weight you carry, you will never find this power."

The two continued through the majestic forest, avoiding the brown-sand path—afraid the enemy would be waiting. As they neared the Second Post, Joe slowed his pace and told Ryan to stay vigilant. Ryan looked through the trees and branches ahead and saw the beautiful entrance to the Second Post. It was a white-squared brick fortress with a twenty-foot door made of shining gold—foreign symbols etched throughout it. As he stared, he heard voices in the distance. Joe grabbed his shoulder and pulled him back. They huddled behind a tree and looked out into the distance.

"It's Haley and the others," Ryan said happily.

Joe quickly calmed Ryan down as he whispered, "Listen—before we go down there, you need to remember that one or more of them are working alongside the enemy. We must be careful. We don't know what we are walking into. If you look at the entrance of the Second Post, there are no guards standing watch, which should never be the case. The enemy has already taken out the lights, so we must be prepared for anything."

At fourteen, Ryan sat nervously in the passenger seat of his father's car with his book bag in his lap. Ryan stayed quiet and shook his leg throughout the drive. The car came to a stop, as they reached their destination. It was his first day of high school, and he was terrified. They parked the car and Ryan's father looked over at Ryan—his nervousness visible. "Things will be a little different than they were back in elementary and middle school. Be prepared for a different way, but as long as you stay true to who you are and be yourself, you will make friends and love high school in no time." His dad leaned over and kissed him on the head. Ryan got off the car, not knowing what to expect, as he went off into a new world.

Ryan and Joe each grabbed a blade, lit them up, and walked out of the forest toward the path. They moved ahead of the group to intercept them before they entered the Second Post. As Ryan and Joe stood waiting, the voices of the group grew louder as they got closer. Ryan could see a light moving in tandem with the group. Tarien was holding a lantern, providing the group with just enough light to see. As they neared, they spotted Ryan and Joe. The group stood still and stared at the two they had assumed were gone.

"No time for small talk," Joe whispered out, "We need to move now."

Haley stepped forward and took the lead, and as she approached them she exchanged a smile with Joe but avoided eye contact with Ryan. His heart sank as she walked right passed him. Tarien and James gave a welcoming handshake to Ryan and Joe. Haley's brothers Eric and Dan followed with Bill. Ian, Landry, and Emily came last, and were smiling from ear to ear, as they came upon Ryan and Joe.

The group marched on to the golden door of the Second Post, which was less than a hundred feet away. As Haley and her brothers led the group, Ryan noticed Ian, Landry, Emily, and Joe whispering to each other. Eavesdropping into their conversation, Ryan overheard their discussion of the potential traitor among the group, as they grabbed weapons out of their bags. Ian held onto a blade, Landry grabbed a bag of crystals, and Emily placed a small round silver ball in her pocket. Tarien held the lantern and provided the light for the group, as they marched on. They arrived at the entrance, taking in its massive golden door with its extraordinary glow and size. On the door were the symbols and signs Ryan had seen throughout his journey, as was the Roman numerical number two. Staring at the entrance, Ryan realized, the door did not contain a handle.

James, as if reading Ryan's mind stated, "Great, so how do we get in without a handle?"

Quickly, Joe spoke up. "Ian, can you work on this?"

Everyone moved aside as Ian walked up to the door and whispered, *"Intrare amicum."* A moment later, a booming noise bellowed out and the door slowly opened. The group stood up in amazement. As Ryan watched the door open, the Key in his pocket shined.

CHAPTER 23

The Second Post

"Joe, can you light up the room?" Tarien said.

Inside the Second Post it was pitch dark. The only illumination came from the lantern now held by Landry and the glow from the blades in Joe and Ian's hands.

"We do not want to let the enemy know we are here," Joe whispered just loudly enough for everyone in the group to hear. "We must try to go unnoticed."

Leading the group, Landry whispered for everyone to follow him inside. From what Ryan could see the ground of the Second Post was made of beautiful brown and white marble and the walls of gold. As they continued, the walls narrowed until they entered a circular room with a waterless fountain in the middle. Within the fountain was a statue of a man kneeling. The group strode passed the fountain looking for the next passageway through the post.

Ian, Landry, and Joe gathered together and discussed their next move. Joe and Landry used the glow from the objects in their possession and shone them around the room. Landry whispered, "I found it." There it was a narrow golden hallway to their right. The group followed the three leaders as they stepped silently to the hallway. The hallway was about fifty feet long and contained foreign symbols along the walls. As they went through the hallway, a loud shriek was heard in the distance from behind them.

"They know we are here," Haley whispered.

Emily snapped her fingers and whispered, "Everyone needs to pick up their pace."

The hallway eventually spilled into another room. This area which was all white was filled with rows of seats.

"Everyone get in," Emily said as the shrieking grew louder.

With everyone inside the room, Emily pulled the silver ball from her pocket. With her index finger she touched it on the top and a ticking sound followed. She pulled her right hand back and rolled the ball down the hallway. "Put your heads down and cover your ears," she whispered. Ryan and the others got behind the seats. Less than five seconds later, a loud blast was heard, and light zoomed into the room from the hallway.

The shrieking sounds ceased as the light was flushed out of the room. Darkness returned, and the only light remained from the blades and the lantern. Sensing they were in the clear, they all came out of hiding. At that moment, a deep and sinister voice yelled out in an unfamiliar language.

"The Dark Shadow is here," Ian whispered to Joe. "Let's move out of this room before we are spotted!"

Once again, the group moved as silently as they could through the next hallway. They quickly reached a small square room. The room was light brown and furnished with desks and chairs, all facing a table in the front made of white crystal marble. The exit from this room consisted of two separate hallways. As Ryan was taking in the beauty of the room—the symbols, the art, the serenity—a beeping noise in the distance was heard inching closer to the group. Joe moved his blade to see what was coming and yelled out, "Get under the desks—now!"

Following Joe's command, they each scrambled to get under a desk. Ryan, Haley, and her brothers were under one; Tarien, James, and Bill under another; and Joe, Emily, Ian, and Landry were under a third. Preparing for what may come; Ryan pulled out the blade from his bag. Noticing Ryan was not with them, Ian and Joe scrambled out from under the desk to be beside Ryan.

"What are you doing?" Ryan whispered.

"When will you realize, we are here to make sure that you make it to the Realm?" Ian whispered back.

As the group remained in hiding, the beeping sound grew louder. As the noise reached its highest pitch, Ryan poked his head out from under the desk and saw a dark metal object with two red beams of light inside, gliding through the air. Discontinuing its movement, the object remained motionless in the air, and the beeping ceased. A second later, the object burst with a deafening sound, triggering the group to cover their ears.

Following the noise, the light from the blades and lanterns were abruptly shut off, leaving the room in complete obscurity. The object traveled around the room, as silence engulfed the area.

"Everyone, be still, and don't make any noise or movements," Landry whispered.

Not heeding the command, Eric and Dan rummaged through their bags. "Be quiet!" Haley whispered.

"I can't see anything. I'm going to put on a light," Dan said. A small light burst from where they were sitting as Dan picked up Ryan's blade.

"What are you doing?" Ryan whispered. As Ryan moved, the bit of light they provided let him see some of the surroundings. When he turned his head to the left, staring back at him was a white and bony human face with fiery eyes—black smoke all around it. Ryan stood still. Haley screamed out in horror. At this sound, the Black Spirit let out a screeching sound and reached out to grab Ryan.

The hand was covered with partial flesh. The human form of the Black Spirit was now more prevalent. As the hand of the Black Spirit neared Ryan, blue crystals flew toward the creature and burst in the air, firing beams of light at the Black Spirit—causing it to disappear. Afterward, chaos ensued. Black Spirits surged into the room as the

Dark Shadow yelled out commands. The group ran toward the two hallways, but with limited visibility, the group split in two, with half going into one exit and the rest in the other.

As they ran down the hallway, Ryan looked back and saw Landry and Joe firing crystals in the air, the explosions lighting up the path in front of the group. The light pierced through the Black Spirits, but now, more humanlike they were able to move faster in and out of the air—landing with their feet on the ground. They relentlessly pursued the group; yet the explosions kept them at bay.

"Look ahead—there is a door to the right," said Bill.

Ahead of them, Ryan could see Haley, Dan, and Bill. Bill was in front and was able to reach the door first and swung it open. As he did, the rest of the group followed and entered the room. "Come on, Joe! Landry, let's go!" Ryan yelled out as the two of them continued to ward off the Black Spirits.

With Ryan holding the door, Joe and Landry successfully held off the Black Spirits and entered the room.

"Shut the door and lock it, quick," Bill shouted.

Just after Ryan locked the door, he could hear shrieks outside.

"They can't come in in here," Joe said. "These walls will protect us."

Completely filled with adrenaline, Ryan replied, "Where is the rest of the group? How do we know they are okay?"

Looking back at Ryan, Landry said, "We have to believe."

Joe turned on a lantern in the room, providing the group with the ability to see their surroundings. The room was filled with chairs and shelves of books like a library. Looking at several of the books, Ryan saw that the shelves were filled with stories of different genres, including sci-fi, romance, sports, and nonfiction.

"Where in the world are we?" he asked out loud.

Picking up one of the books, Joe responded, "We are in a waiting room."

"Waiting for what?" Bill asked.

Joe put down the book and sat in a chair. "To enter into the Realm."

CHAPTER 24

Waiting Game

The group was in the room for nearly an hour, listening to the Black Spirits outside the door attempting to locate a way in. As Ryan sat quietly, he heard Haley crying in the back. Ryan grabbed a chair and went over to try and console her.

"Haley, are you okay?" he asked.

Dan, who never had much to say, got up from his chair and angrily stated, "She is fine. Let her be."

Haley picked her head up and, with tears rolling down her cheeks, said, "Something is wrong, Ryan. I have not been feeling like myself since we entered the forest. Then I had the most awful dream when I was sleeping." Unsure of what to say, Ryan continued to listen. "I don't know where Dylan is, and I just have this feeling that something bad is going to happen. And then the strangest thing of all is this." She reached to grab her bag from under a chair and stuck her hand inside. What she pulled out of it was most unusual—a small pink stuffed bear.

"A teddy bear?" Ryan asked in befuddlement.

"No. Not just a teddy bear, she is Ms. Huggy. This was my favorite thing in the whole world as little girl. I would go everywhere with Ms. Huggy. No matter how bad things were at home, she was always by my side."

She handed the bear over to Ryan, still confused. "So you brought it with you?" he asked.

"See, that's the thing. I didn't pack this bag. It was given to me before I entered the Blue Alley. And that is not the only item in there. There are other toys, pictures, clothes, books, and games that were all my favorite things growing up. Most of these were thrown away a long time ago or lost."

At a loss for words, Ryan just sat there next to Haley as she put her head on his shoulder. In the back, he could hear Dan muttering of how childish his sister was acting.

Two hours passed, and the group grew anxious inside the room. Joe and Landry stood up and faced the others. "We need to get out of here. We haven't heard anything outside for over a half hour, and we need to get to the Realm as soon as possible," Landry said, specifically eyeing Ryan. Landry and Joe made eye contact and nodded.

"Okay, everyone needs to grab their bag and get ready to run when given the word," Joe said, his tone serious. "Landry is going to distract them, and we will need to get through the portal ahead. Do not be frightened when you see it. Just keep on going and you will land into the last stretch of the Blue Alley."

Haley stood up. "What do you mean Landry is going to distract them?" she asked. "How is he going to stop them all by himself?"

Landry pulled out objects from his bag and replied, "Don't worry about me. This is what I came for."

"This is crazy!" Bill shouted. "We will be sitting ducks once we go outside." Joe asked him to lower his voice.

Dan was the next to speak out. "We can't wait here any longer."

The group eventually came to terms with the plan, as they grabbed their bags, and anxiously waited for the door to swing open.

CHAPTER 25

The Portal

Landry opened the door as slowly and quietly as possible. The group waited in a line behind Joe. The tension grew thicker with each passing moment. Ryan grabbed his blade and held onto it firmly as Landry stuck his head out from behind the door to see out—darkness was on both sides of the hallway. "Everyone ready?" he whispered and grabbed two black grenade-like items. He paused, breathed in, and said, "Let's do this." He tossed one grenade in the direction they had come from and one toward the direction they were headed. Moments after each was tossed, lights burst without noise through the hallway and into the room.

"Let's go," Joe said.

The silence in this hallway gave Ryan chills all over his body. Holding tight to his blade, Ryan followed Joe, who carried a lantern in his left hand and crystals in his right. As they moved, Ryan kept a close eye on Haley, who was behind Joe and was in front of Dan and Bill. Ryan glanced back and saw Landry trailing the group, looking around for any sign of the enemy. Continuing, Ryan observed various doors on both sides of the hallway; wondering where they led. As they neared the end of the hallway, they heard a familiar noise: the sound of flowing waterfalls.

The end of the hallway led into another cave-like area with waterfalls all around. There was a beautiful circular drawing on the floor in the middle of the cave. By the light from the lanterns and blades, they were able to see the drawing—a beautiful sunset with a crystal blue sky and orange seeping through from the setting sun. As the group entered, the pace slowed down. Ahead of them, connected to the painting on the floor, was a narrow bridge that led to an immense square screen. The screen was made of white moving liquid.

"Is that the Portal?" Ryan asked. "How do we go through it?"

Joe walked over to the screen and put his right hand up to touch the liquid-filled Portal. His hand went right through it. "You see? Nothing to be afraid of," he said.

Suddenly, the room went dark, as the light from the lantern and blades were once again abruptly shut off.

Panic set in as the group heard the Black Spirits making their way toward them.

"Ryan, it is time for you to decide where you stand," the whispering voice said.

"Someone turn on a light!" Haley yelled out.

As shrieks surrounded the group, Landry grabbed a small canister from his bag and placed it on the floor. Moments later the canister lit up with a small white glow, providing limited visibility for the group. Ryan looked around to see where everyone was. He could not locate Joe, until he looked all the way to his left and there he was—floating in the air at the hand of the Dark Shadow was Joe. The Dark Shadow had entered the room unnoticed. The creature was of a large frame—that of an eight foot man. It had a fiery body that was draped with a black coat and black smoke surrounding it. The Dark Shadow raised its hand up toward Joe. As he moved his hand, Joe's body jerked in the direction of his hand. Joe was a puppet and the Dark Shadow his puppeteer.

"Landry, please do something!" Ryan shouted.

More shrieks came from the Black Spirits as the sounds of them coming in and out of the air neared the group.

"We can't leave him!" Ryan shouted.

"It's okay, Ryan. You have to go," Joe said, trying with all his might to speak as his body was being crushed by the grip of the Dark Shadow.

As Ryan went to motion Landry for help, he turned around to see Landry's lifeless body slowly collapse to the ground. Standing above Landry's body was Dan—grinning with a blade in his hand. Landry's body evaporated swiftly into blue, twirling dust which spiraled upward.

"What have you done?" Haley yelled frantically. "What have you done?!"

With a sinister tone, Dan responded, "I had to choose a side, and I decided to go with the one who will eventually control everything." He turned his sights on Ryan and said, "You have been given chances to join, but now you will suffer the same fate as the rest of them."

At Dan's words, Ryan's rage arose. He kept his eyes on Dan, who strolled over to stand next to the Dark Shadow. From the corner of his eye, he saw Joe on the floor, out of the grasp of the Dark Shadow and gasping for air. Three Black Spirits appeared in front of Joe.

"Bill, take Haley through the portal now," Ryan said with conviction as he stared at the Black Spirits gathering upon Joe.

"Ryan, I am not going to leave without you again!" Haley shouted as Bill forcefully yanked her toward the Portal. As Haley screamed out to Ryan, she and Bill vanished through the liquid portal. Suddenly a Black Spirit appeared in front of Ryan. With its decrepit hand and smoke all around, it reached out and tossed Ryan's body against the cave wall.

"Champ? Champ? Are you okay?" Ryan's father said as Ryan lay in the outfield of his high school baseball field. With his baseball uniform on and a throbbing pain piercing his knees, Ryan asked, "Where are we, Dad? I don't remember this ever happening."

Ryan's father kneeled down on the floor next to him and said, "Champ, we are nearing the final inning. I know you are hurting, but it's time for you to rise. You were meant to be a leader. So lead. Get up, son. Get up!"

Ryan's eyes opened wide, and in front of him was the Black Spirit. Still on the floor, Ryan felt a sense of peace inside that he had not had since the passing of his father. As the Black Spirit began a motion of attack, Ryan stood on his feet with energy brimming through him. He felt a sense of power inside his body unlike anything he had felt before. With this newfound feeling, Ryan leaned back slightly, and with the memory of Landry in his mind, he flung his arms toward the Black Spirit. He thrusted a wave of air and an explosion of energy toward the enemy—each of the Black Spirits in the room were blown back. Ryan looked down at his hands, not believing what he had just done.

"Help me," Joe said, struggling on the floor. Ryan quickly went over to Joe, helped him up, and walked over to the Portal. Right as they were about to make their way through, Ryan was hit from behind—as if he had been struck by a baseball bat—causing him to collapse. In agony, he looked up and saw the Dark Shadow yelling commands. As Ryan struggled to get back up, a Black Spirit rushed toward Joe. Ryan quickly gathered himself and thrust his hands forward, releasing a blast of air. This time, however, the air ripped through the Black Spirit—shredding it into black dust. At that moment, Ryan grabbed Joe, and before the Dark Shadow could muster any power, he and Joe entered the Portal.

Images began to appear before his eyes—visions encompassing his life. His memories began to play out right in front of him like a movie, moving in chronological order: spending time with his parents and their friends at the beach on a small island called the Sandile, playing sports, his dad coaching him, going to the movies, eating dinner and attending sporting events with his dad, driving back from his games with his father and replaying each moment, winning a district baseball game and seeing the look on his father's face, hugging his father, listening to his dad tell him how proud he was of him—and, finally, reliving the horrifying events that had played out only months ago when his father had passed away. The visions poured out in front of Ryan, recreating the story of his life. As Ryan was looking on at his father's casket, he felt a cool breeze on his skin and light penetrating his eyelids.

CHAPTER 26

The Beach

As Ryan opened his eyes, he gazed out at the most spectacular beach and sunset he had ever seen. The calm water was as clear as a pool, and the sand was powder white. Scattered throughout the sand were beautiful palm trees. He looked around and observed that the beach was inside of a dome. The sand to his left went a hundred feet to the tip of the water, while to his right the sand hit a light blue wall—it contained the same foreign symbols and writings he'd seen throughout his journey. Scanning his new surroundings, he saw Joe sitting to his left. Ryan gathered himself, walked over to Joe, and assisted him to his feet.

"Joe are you okay? Where are we now?" an awe-inspired Ryan asked.

Joe, fighting off the pain he was in, replied, "Look out in the distance. What do you see?"

Ryan, who had been focusing on the beauty of the beach, had not realized what was straight ahead of him in the distance: it was a colossal castle of shimmering gold stretching out both in length and width as far as Ryan could see. The architecture was astounding, as it appeared to be made of rocks and stones, yet it looked as sturdy as any fortress.

"What is that?" Ryan asked.

"That, my friend, is the Realm!" Joe responded. "Help me get to that palm tree over there so I can catch my breath," Joe said, trying to regain his strength.

"Don't we need to get to the Realm before the Devamans come through the Portal?" Ryan asked as they moved toward the tree.

Wincing in pain, Joe replied, "They won't be able to find their way through for a little while, as the only one who could possibly come through is Dan, but he wouldn't come alone, knowing that we now know what side he is on."

It took them a minute to reach a full-sized, vibrant green palm tree. Ryan helped Joe sit down and joined him. As the two sat facing the sunset and crystal blue water, a group of six white birds flew through the air and Ryan realized that the painting he had just seen by the Portal was now the image in front of him. It truly was a spectacular vision. He turned his attention to the magnificence of the Realm and said, "I am ready to finally listen to you, Joe. I am ready to embrace this place and believe."

Joe stared at Ryan with his usual serious demeanor and said, "It's about time."

Now intent on listening to Joe's message, Ryan asked, "Where is the rest of the group? And why aren't Haley and Bill here?"

Joe adjusted himself on the ground to get comfortable and replied, "They are all more than likely at the third and final post, which is right before the entrance of the Realm. That entrance is where we need to get you, so you can stop the Devamans from entering the Realm by turning the Key. The only one who can turn the Key is you, as it was given to you and no one else. This is the way the Realm was created. You are a Keeper, someone not from this place, who, when the time requires, can ensure our safety and survival."

Trying to process the information, Ryan asked, "What did I do by the Portal to stop the Devamans? All of a sudden this rush of energy and force flowed through me."

Joe looked up at Ryan and said, "Since you are not part of this world, you are able to manipulate the energy inside the Blue Alley solely by focusing your mind. The power you have here is unlimited, but it can only be harnessed if you are able to clear your mind and learn to believe in who you are. We now know Dan compromised the Blue Alley, so it's only a matter of time until he and the rest of the Devamans come through. As you saw, the Dark Shadow is also able to manipulate energy as well. I was hoping to teach all of this to you sooner, but you were not ready."

As Joe slowly picked himself up from the ground, he asked Ryan what had come over him by the Portal that gave him the ability to use his strength. Remembering the vision of his father urging him on, he replied, "I just closed my eyes, and someone close to me gave me the strength."

And with Joe's usual matter-of-fact demeanor, he said, "Then let's get to work."

CHAPTER 27

Letting Go

As they made their way to the beach water, Joe asked Ryan to toss a shell from the ground in front of them into the water, using only the energy around him. Focused on this impossible idea, Ryan stared at the shell for a minute, but nothing happened. He glanced back at Joe with a face of defeat. "Close your eyes and concentrate. Find your gift," Joe said quietly. Ryan obeyed and shut his eyes.

Ryan was in a dark room walking toward a shiny black object in the distance ahead. As he moved forward, he heard what sounded like crying. He looked around but no one was there.

"Hello? Who is there? What's wrong?" he shouted—no one answered. He felt a cold chill come over his body as the temperature in the room plummeted. All he could hear were his footsteps striking the floor. As he got closer to the object, he realized what it was. It was a closed casket. He looked around the room again but saw nothing. It was dark all over, except for a light shining over the casket. Five feet away from the casket, the room began to feel unbearably hot. Eventually, he stood in front of the casket and reached his hand out to open it. Terrified of what was inside, his hands trembled. There was a creaking noise as the lid of the casket opened. Ryan glanced inside the casket and what was in there caused his legs to buckle.

A dizzy feeling swarmed over him. The body inside the casket was his own. He reached out to grab the folded hands in the casket and as he held them, he thought of how cold and wooden they felt. His body in the casket was completely pale. He fell to his knees, and shook the body. "Wake up! Wake up! This is all a dream. You can't be dead." As he continued to move the body, the casket swayed. Shortly thereafter, the casket fell over and his body tumbled out.

"Ryan! Ryan, snap out of it!" Ryan opened his eyes and felt a stream of tears flowing down his face. He looked over to Joe and said, "I can't do this! There is too much pain inside."

Joe put his hand on Ryan's shoulder. "You have months of anger and sadness trapped in you that won't let you breathe."

Ryan stood up frustrated and moved to where the water met the sand. He grabbed a shell with his right hand, tossed into the water, and said, "I don't know how."

Joe calmly went over and said, "Try again."

Ryan was terrified to close his eyes, but he trusted Joe. He hesitantly obliged.

He was back in the same room he had just left, kneeling on the cold floor. In front of him was the fallen casket. Frantically, he looked around the room to find his body, but could not locate it. He started to sweat uncontrollably as the room appeared to be closing in on him. On his knees and completely distraught, he felt a hand on his shoulder. At that moment, he closed his eyes, terrified of what or who was behind him. With the hand still on his shoulder, he slowly turned his head to the right. Moving his head to look up, he saw his father smiling down at him. "Stand up, Champ," his father said, extending his hand to help Ryan off the floor.

Ryan stood up and looked at his father. "Dad, what am I supposed to do? How do I become this person they believe me to be?"

His father came up to Ryan and whispered, "There is nothing to fear, son. I am right by your side."

Ryan opened his eyes to the beach—this time, however, he felt a sense of power. He pushed his right hand out toward the shoreline—a rock by the water swayed. With greater focus and concentration, he whispered, "This is for you Dad." As the words rolled out of his mouth, the rock was flung across the water. As the rock skipped across, Ryan looked down at his hands and up at Joe.

With a smirk, Joe said, "I told you, kid! It's inside you!"

Not done testing his newfound strength, Ryan focused once more. This time he opened his right hand, his palm facing the sand below, and closed his eyes. With Joe looking on, Ryan's hand shook, and the sand below slowly rose. Grain by grain, the sand elevated up towards Ryan's hand. As the sand lifted, Ryan moved his hand in a circular motion—the sand twirled. He opened his eyes and witnessed the movement of the sand, and in this moment, he was no longer surprised by his abilities. He continued the motion until he thrust his hands forward, unleashing a powerful blast of air toward the water and sending a shockwave with it. He turned to Joe and proclaimed, "I am ready."

CHAPTER 28

The Third Post

As Joe and Ryan trekked toward the Third Post, a thundering sound was heard coming from the direction of the Portal.

"Joe, what is that?" Ryan asked.

Joe looked back at the Portal and said, "We have about ten to fifteen minutes before a war begins. The Devamans are coming."

They walked along the water, and as they neared the Realm, Ryan was impressed by its size and blown away by its magnificence. He had never appreciated the beauty in any structure he had ever seen as he did now.

As they reached the entrance of the final post, Ryan's pocket glowed brighter than ever before. The post did not contain a door; instead, the entrance consisted of two beautiful concrete beams with the Roman numerical number three and a carved lettering that read, *"Finis de iter itineris."* The beams were connected to white tile walls which went up nearly fifteen feet, and extended a good distance on both sides. There were two guards stationed at the entrance, each holding a metal pole with spears on both ends. The guards went over to Joe and discussed a plan of action. As the conversation concluded, one of the guards ran inside the Third Post, and within seconds, an alarm siren blasted through the air. Thirty guards came rushing to the entrance with spears in their hands, facing the direction of the Portal.

"Hendricks, I will be back in a minute," Joe told one of the initial two guards. Joe motioned Ryan to follow. As they entered, Ryan looked at the Third Post—there were no buildings or extra walkways. A small simple wooden shed was seen to his left, with guards exiting with artillery in hand. There were benches and tables to his right. Ryan watched on, as the guards requested everyone inside the post to make their way to the entrance of the Realm. As he observed the nervousness in the voice of the guards, Ryan felt a warm hand on his shoulder. He turned around—it was Haley. She leaped into his arms and embraced him. He closed his eyes and breathed a sigh of relief.

"I hope we get a hug like that next!" Tarien whispered to James, Emily, Eric, and Ian. "It's great to see you again," soft-spoken Emily said.

Ryan turned to Haley and inquired as to how she was doing. "I still can't believe that my brother betrayed us," she quickly responded. Eric, at the sound of hearing his brother's name, entered the conversation and, with anger in his voice, said his brother would pay. Tarien and James came in and softened the mood with their usual humor as they spoke of the Realm and of how Bill, Cooper, and his mother had already entered.

Out of the corner of his eye, Ryan saw Emily, Ian and Joe gathered together several feet away. Turning back to the group, he said, "Listen we don't have much time before the Devamans get here. They want to get into the Realm and won't stop at anything to do so. It's time for each of you to seek shelter inside the Realm. I am going to stay and fight."

They looked around at each other until Haley said, "I am not going into the Realm without you." She said this with such passion as she reached to grab Ryan's hand.

"Wait—you think after all this, we would leave you? That we would not stay and fight with you and Joe to keep this place safe?

You must be crazy," Tarien blurted out as James shook his head in agreement.

"My brother will not get away with this. So I am staying," Eric vehemently replied.

As they each spoke out, Ryan looked around, and for the first time in a long time, felt the warmth of friendship.

As the group stood staring up at the Realm, Joe and Ian came over and asked to speak with Ryan alone. Ryan obliged, as they separated from the rest of the group.

"We overheard your conversation, and we are thankful that you want to stay and fight, but right now we need you to go through that marble door attached to the Realm entrance and turn the Key." Ian said as he pointed ahead to a door in the distance which was camouflaged into an immense marble wall which connected to the Realm entrance.

Before Ian could finish his words, Ryan shook his head in disapproval. "I thought you needed me to help fight them off. I thought I had these powers so I could help stop the Devamans,"

"This is still true, Ryan," Joe said. "Without understanding your powers, the Key could never turn. You are the one who will save us but not in battle. By turning the Key, you will flood the Blue Alley walls with a blanket of energy that will be impenetrable for the next fifty years and will lock down the doors to the Realm." Joe gestured for one of the guards to come over. "Charles, please make sure that Ryan is taken to the marble door."

As Joe said this, reverberations were once again heard coming in the direction of the Portal. Ryan looked out and dark, ominous clouds were seen forming.

"Joe, you need my help to stop them," Ryan defiantly proclaimed.

Joe put his hand out to shake Ryan's and said, "Good luck, kid. We will hold them off to give you enough time."

Finishing their good-byes, Joe and Ian walked hastily toward the entrance of the post and grabbed a set of spears. Confused of what he should do, Ryan felt Charles nudge him on his back to move forward. Ryan dismissed Charles and walked over to Haley and the rest of the group. As quickly as he could he explained his task of turning the Key and pleaded for them to get inside the Realm. The group refused to leave without him.

"We enter all as one!" James stated.

With a look of determination, Haley said, "We will hold them off and go in together."

"Go, Ryan. We will be fine," Tarien said.

After each of them wished Ryan good luck, they made their way to the entrance of the Third Post and prepared for battle, as in the distance the Dark Shadow and Black Spirits made their way through the portal and onto the beach.

CHAPTER 29

Darkness Comes

The light in the distance grew obscure as a storm brewed. The Dark Shadow and its army of Black Spirits marched toward the Realm. Making his way to the marble door, Ryan looked back and saw lightning in the distance, creeping closer to the entrance of the Third Post. He was torn inside: should he turn the Key or help his friends in battle? Each step he took toward the door tormented him—he felt as if he was walking in slow motion. Sweat slid down his forehead as he reached the door. The door, veiled by the surrounding wall, had a white handle. As he stood in front of it, he admired the striking marble and the cracks around it which seemed intentionally placed.

"Ryan, once the door is opened, I cannot go inside. Only the one with the Key may enter," Charles said.

Ryan could not concentrate on the words coming out of Charles, as an explosion was heard in the distance. Ryan turned his body and stared out toward the post entrance. The enemy was approaching the guards as immense lightning bolts danced across the sky, followed by thunderous blasts. At that moment, Ryan looked down at the Key in his hands and closed his eyes for a second. When he opened them, wide-eyed, he yelled out, "I'm sorry, Charles! I'm not leaving them to die." He placed the Key back in his pocket and sprinted toward the entrance as the tide of darkness was staring him straight ahead. He now knew what he had to do—it was time to fight.

As he raced to the entrance, the area was covered by a thick black fog. The wind was swirling, and Ryan could not see out into the distance. As he arrived at the entrance, he heard loud booming sounds. He stood still and looked up. Ten separate streams of light were shot up into the air from metal rods burrowed into the ground and manned by guards. Once a stream of light was sent up, a guard would place a blue tube into the rod and light a fire at the bottom of the rod—out would burst bolts of light which lit up the beach. With the light crashing through the fog, Ryan saw hundreds of Black Spirits making their way toward the entrance.

With streams of lights illuminating his surroundings, Ryan looked around to find the group. To his right he saw Haley, Tarien, James, and Eric, each with a single spear in their hands—a bright glow coming from the tip of the spears. In front of them were Ian and Joe with double-sided spears with white light beaming on both sides. As Ryan walked over to the group, the stream of lights exploded in the air, and as they did, each one multiplied into a vast strip of arrows.

As the arrows filled with a fiery glow, spiraled downward toward the Black Spirits, a voice shouted, "Ryan, what are you doing back here? You are not supposed to be here." It was Emily.

"I will not leave you all. Once I know everyone is safe, I will turn the Key," Ryan replied as he continued moving.

Haley was the first to see Ryan. As she turned to tell the others, the glowing arrows glided down like darts toward the Black Spirits whose human characteristics were more prevalent. With the arrows barreling toward them, many of the Black Spirits moved in and out of the air in time to avoid being pierced. Yet, the immense lights were able to puncture through and pulverize a vast majority of the Black Spirits into dust.

"Ryan, what are you doing here?" Haley asked.

Ryan looked at Haley and the others and replied, "No chance I was going to let you all fight alone and get all the glory."

Tarien and James patted Ryan on the back and Haley smiled. Ian and Joe were ready to argue with Ryan, but the battle was already raging on.

As the Devamans prepared their next assault, guards ushered over hefty black poles that were connected at the top to a brown circular metal ring. The poles were manned by two guards and had levers at the bottom. As the levers were wound by the guards, blue and white sparks of electricity formed inside the circular rings. The electricity intensified and was accompanied by static. "Release them!" Joe yelled out. With this command, the guards let go of the levers, and the circular rings on each pole shot out a ball of electricity toward the incoming Black Spirits. Once the electricity was in front of the Black Spirits, its movement stopped. As the electricity was suspended in the air in front of them, the Black Spirits, with their half flesh bodies and trailing smoke, ceased their movement. Then, without notice, the electricity exploded outward toward the enemy. The Black Spirits were able to vanish in the air in time to avoid the piercing light. When they reappeared several feet forward or behind the explosion, they did not expect what followed. The eruption sent a burst of energy out and created a silver circular hole suspended in the air. Within several seconds, all of the energy released and anything surrounding it was sucked into the hole. Hundreds of Black Spirits were swallowed into the hole, shrieking as they vanished. Moments later, the energy and everything else inside detonated into tiny particles. The remaining few Black Spirits retreated and the guards celebrated this victory.

Haley, Ryan, Tarien, James, and Eric rejoiced at the victory. As they were celebrating, Ryan looked over at Joe and Ian, and did not see the same joy in their faces. Joe tried to yell out to the guards to stay alert, but the cheering and chatter drowned out his voice. Sensing something was wrong; Ryan stared at Joe and tried to read his lips. As Joe repeated the same phrase over and over, Ryan was able to figure it out. "Get ready! They are coming back."

A lightning strike hurled through the Third Post. As Ryan stared ahead, the whispering voice returned in his ear. "This is the end for everything," the voice whispered. "Ryan, follow my voice. It is time we join forces."

At that moment, Haley looked over at Ryan and knew something was off. His eyes, containing a red glow, were wide-open. He was facing the rising darkness, and he began to mumble. When Haley attempted to snap him out of his trance, he muttered out, "They took him from me." Unfazed by Haley, Ryan marched toward the evil ahead. As he did, a large bolt of lightning lit up the area, revealing the Dark Shadow ahead. With visible fire moving throughout the inside of its body, the Dark Shadow stood in the open sand, flanked by a large swarm of Black Spirits.

"Joe! Ian!" Haley yelled.

By now, Ryan was outside the battle fence created by the guards and was headed toward the Dark Shadow.

"Ryan, it's time to pay back those who have hurt you. We will do it together."

Ryan, locked into the voice, continued forward. At that moment, Joe jumped over the fence, rushed toward Ryan, and tackled him to the ground.

"Remember who you are! Remember!" Joe said as he held Ryan down. "Your father told me who you are. And he has told me to tell you he loves you," Joe yelled out in a last-ditch effort to bring Ryan back. As he said this, Ryan lay motionless and the red glow faded from his eyes as they closed.

CHAPTER 30

Stand Tall, Stand Strong

Ryan opened his eyes and saw Joe standing over him. "Are you okay, Ryan?" he asked. Unsure of how he'd ended up in the sand and away from the post, he said yes. As Joe helped Ryan to his feet, there was a loud explosion followed by a blast of air and sand, knocking Joe and Ryan down to the floor. The burst of air toppled the fence, the guards, and the weapons stationed by the Third Post. As Ryan gathered himself, he looked back to see a surge of thick black smoke heading in the direction of the post. With it came an upwelling of Black Spirits moving in and out of the air and the Dark Shadow close behind.

As the Devamans charged forward, Ryan and Joe regained their footing and looked out in horror at the force with which the Black Spirits were moving toward them—fading in and out of vision. Ryan turned to Joe and saw in his hands, a small rectangular detonator. Joe straightened up, looking on as the Black Spirits charged forward. He breathed in one time and pressed the yellow button in the middle of the detonator. Bolts of light sprang up from the ground ahead of them as the Black Spirits were met with land mines set up throughout the sand. Able to sense when a Black Spirit was near, the land mines thrust light up into the air—dissolving them into dust.

"Okay, I bought us some time to get back to the fence," Joe proclaimed. The two ran back to the fence, while the screams of the Black Spirits, burning from the bolts of light, echoed in the distance.

As they reached the fence, Joe observed the guards who were trying to gather themselves from the blast. A worthy portion of their artillery had been destroyed. As he looked upon them, Joe yelled out. "The time has come for us all to stand up against this evil! We have trained for this day, and it is now here. We cannot let them take away our home—our home, which has opened its arms for centuries. Stand tall. Stand strong. And stand together. This is the side of good, and it's time we fight for it."

In unison, the guards shouted in approval, "For the Realm!"

Joe yelled out one final command: "Get ready, and let's give them one last battle!"

In all the commotion, Ryan searched for Haley and the others. In the distance, he spotted Haley, and for the first time in a long time, a big smile spread across Ryan's face. As he neared her, she ran and lunged into his arms. He held her tight and closed his eyes, and his mind was clear. He was in the moment, and the moment was about Haley.

"You really scared me there. I thought we had lost you," she whispered to him.

"I'm not going anywhere," he whispered back.

"Okay, love birds. Relax," a joyful James came up and said. The group shared a moment of happiness and friendship, but it was short-lived, as the ground beneath them rumbled and an immense black canvas of smoke barreled towards them.

"Grab your spears!" Ian yelled out. "Stay back and be ready to use them."

The ground shook ferociously and the wind swirled as the force of evil grew intensely around them. The lights from the tips of the spears provided them with minimal illumination as darkness enraptured the Third Post.

The ground started to crack. The guards pointed their spears toward the darkness ahead, waiting for the Black Spirits to emerge. As they stood, one by one the guards vanished. The only sounds heard were their screams as they disappeared into the blackness.

"Everyone back up and point the light toward the ground ahead!" Joe yelled out.

As they did, ten black tentacles were seen squirming back into a sizeable hole in the terrain in front of the guards.

"Stay alert everyone," Ian yelled out.

Ryan and the group huddled together behind the guards. As Ryan looked forward, two guards in front of him were lifted up from the ground. As the guards were suspended in the air, everyone stood and watched in horror. Seconds later, the bodies of the guards were crushed and dissolved into a blue dust. Ahead, Ryan saw the fiery eyes of the Dark Shadow, its power stronger than ever.

Sensing a weakness, the Devamans sent out a full attack against the guards. The creature from the ground unleashed its tentacles—reaching for anything it could find. As the tentacles moved farther out, its body was revealed. It was an octopus-like creature, filled with fire and the faces of Black Spirits inside its belly. The creature continued forward, reaching for any prey it could find.

"Fire away!" Joe yelled.

At that moment, the guards unleashed bolts of light from their spears toward the creature.

"Aim for the body!" Ian yelled. Hundreds of bolts crashed into the creature.

Eventually too many blows of light caused the body of the creature to explode. The explosion unleashed fire specks from inside its body towards the guards and burning their skin.

As the assault from the Devamans continued, the Black Spirits disappeared and reappeared in front of the guards, who were battling the onslaught with their double-sided spears. Ryan turned to Ian and Joe and was amazed by the speed with which they were handling their spears and warding off the Black Spirits. They used their spears as swords and tossed light out at the same time. They annihilated each Black Spirit that attacked them. Though they were holding their own, the remaining guards were not as lucky as the Black Spirits, moving quicker, lunged at the guards, barreling through their bodies.

As the battle raged on, Haley yelled out, "Ryan, what is that heading our way?"

Ryan pulled his gaze away from the battle and saw a wave of sand in the distance rising in height and moving toward them. "It is coming right at us!" Tarien shouted. With the sand increasing in speed, Ryan put his hands out, closed his eyes, and unleashed energy from within. As he closed and opened his fists toward the oncoming danger, the ground ahead began to crack and split open. As the sand neared, it was unable to reach them, as it tumbled down into the crevasse created by Ryan.

As the sand fell, a twenty-foot thick black snake rushed out of the sand, grabbing onto Tarien's legs. It wrapped around Tarien's body and began to slither away. As they stared helplessly, three bolts of light shot through the air and pierced the snake, causing it to release its grip on Tarien. Ryan looked over his right shoulder and saw Emily with a spear in her hand pointed toward the snake. "Turn around!" Emily yelled out to Ryan. As he did, the body of the snake transformed into black smoke, twirling in the air until it formed the fiery body of the Dark Shadow.

With smoke circling it, the Dark Shadow raised its right hand and absorbed the energy around it. A ring of fire formed inside its palm. The group stared at the sight of the fire swarming together in its hand. Before Ryan could react, the Dark Shadow thrust its hand forward, launching the energy toward Ryan. With the fire beaming toward him, Ryan tried to deflect the energy away. However, the speed at which it came towards him was too fast for Ryan to move out of its path. Ryan closed his eyes and succumbed to the idea that this was the end.

With his eyes closed, he waited for the fire to crash through him, but it did not. All he heard was a woman's voice scream out in front of him. When he opened his eyes, he looked down and saw her lying on the ground, her body badly burnt—Emily. He immediately bent down to help her. As he kneeled in front of her, he reached out for her hand. Bolts of light flashed by Ryan toward the Dark Shadow, as Ian and Joe unleashed an assault. Warding off the attack, the Dark Shadow created a dark liquid force field ahead of it; deflecting the oncoming light. Then without noticed, the Dark Shadow disappeared, leaving a trail of smoke.

Ryan focused on Emily as she spoke to him in a soft voice. "Ryan, thank goodness you're okay!"

Ryan could not believe she had risked her life for him. "I am okay only because of you. Why did you do that?"

With her last breath, Emily replied, "My sweet boy that is why I am here. That is why we came here: to guide you and keep you safe. How you have grown, my boy."

Before Ryan could reply, Emily's body disintegrated into dust and swirled up into the air.

CHAPTER 31

The Power Within

Still on his knees, Ryan felt a hand on his shoulder—it was Haley. She attempted to console him, but at this point Ryan was tired of saying good-bye. With Joe and Ian by his side, firing off bolts of light at the Black Spirits, Ryan stood up and with all the power inside he could muster, thrust his hands forward. This sent an intense gust of wind, knocking away anything in its path. He turned to his left, where there were guards fighting off a group of Black Spirits.

"Joe, let me have your spear," Ryan firmly stated.

Joe did as he was asked. With the spear in his left hand, Ryan put his right hand over the glow from the spear and closed his eyes. As he did, the glow from the spear dimmed and his body began to absorb the light. Everyone around him stood in awe as his arm glowed with light and his eyes contained a crystal blue radiance. With perfect precision, he hurled bolts of light from his hands; piercing through the remaining Black Spirits. As the last of the Blacks Spirits disintegrated, Ryan fell to his knees, yelled aloud, and punched the ground with his two fists, sending the energy within him out in a wave of light hurling forward, dissolving any Black Spirit remaining on the beach.

"They are gone!" Haley said as she kneeled down next to him. Ryan kept his head down until he felt the light creeping back into the beach and the darkness faded into the distance. A hand reached down to help Ryan off the ground—it was Joe. Right behind him was Ian; both with wounds covering their face and body.

"Emily—she is gone," Ryan said as he stood up.

"I know, Ryan," Ian said. "But she completed her mission."

Finding it odd how calm Ian was as he said this, Ryan was thrown off by the sound of Eric's yelling out.

"You are unbelievable! Everywhere you go, bad things happen and death follows. It's time that you pay for once."

When Ryan looked in the direction of Eric's voice, he saw a guard collapse to the ground in pain. Standing on top of the fallen body was another guard who was holding onto a spear.

"Dan!" Haley yelled. "Why are you doing this?"

Dan, posing as a guard, laughed out loud. "You all think you're better than me. You will all suffer in the face of the darkness."

Eric, enraged, ran toward Dan, who now had noticeable trail of smoke following him. His body was growing thinner and scrawnier, as was he transforming into a Black Spirit. Continuing to laugh as Eric neared him, Dan was able to quickly avoid his brother, who fell to the ground.

"Ryan, you think that this over?" Dan said with evil in his eyes. "The dark never sleeps."

Dan forcefully grabbed Eric from the ground and held him from behind, his right arm around Eric's neck. As he held Eric, Dan yelled out, "Sorry, Haley, but we chose our path a long time ago, and ours is on the other side."

With a surge of smoke, the Dark Shadow appeared out of thin air. At that moment, Ryan attempted to create enough strength to save Eric, but the Dark Shadow made the first move, waving its arms toward Tarien and lifting him into the air. Suspended in the air, Tarien began to hyperventilate as the life was being sucked out of him. Ryan thrust all of the energy inside of him toward the Dark

Luis Vazquez-Bello

Shadow, but before the wave of energy could reach it, the Dark Shadow created a force field, protecting itself, Dan, and Eric. With the force field up, the Dark Shadow dropped Tarien to the ground, and dark smoke engulfed Eric and Dan. Within seconds, their bodies along with the Dark Shadow vanished.

"They are gone," Haley cried out, as tears flowed down. "They are gone! Where did they go?"

CHAPTER 32

The Last Stand

Ryan consoled Haley, until Joe and Ian approached and told him it was time for him to turn the Key. The guards and group members who had survived trekked toward the entrance of the Realm. Ryan held onto Haley's hand as they moved toward the Realm. As they walked, Ryan looked back and noticed Joe and Ian whispering to each other and staring at Ryan and Haley. Ryan, not paying much attention to them, turned to a disheartened Haley and said, "When we get into the Realm, I'm sure your mother will be there waiting with Dylan. It will all be alright."

As they walked into the Third Post, an immense rumbling was heard in the distance. "Are you serious? When will this end?" James yelled out in frustration.

The ground beneath the group started to move uncontrollably, and as they turned back, a giant wave of red, fiery sand could be seen bursting toward them. Unlike before, this wave of sand contained flames firing off on all sides and a deafening shriek. Seeing the oncoming danger, anyone who remained in the Third Post raced toward the entrance of the Realm. As he ran, Ryan looked back and noted Black Spirits entangled in the fiery sand. Ryan could hear the guards behind him, engulfed by the flames. Tarien and James led the way forward, followed by Ryan, Haley, Joe, and Ian.

As they neared the Realm, Ryan could feel the sand beneath his shoes boiling. At that moment, he knew that they would not make it inside. He stopped his sprint, turned around, and closed his eyes. "Help me, dad," he whispered. He breathed in, opened his eyes, and moved his right hand in a circular motion. As he did, the sand in front of him spun up into the air. He moved his hand faster, and the sand continued to rise—wind followed. With the fiery sand barreling down on them, Ryan with all of his might sent the sand and wind blasting toward the oncoming fire. As the wind collided with the sand, the fire was immobilized in its track and rushed upward. The shrieking noise reached a fever pitch as the fire faded away.

As the fire disappeared into the ground, black smoke rose up. With the beauty of the Realm to their back, the group faced the smoke as it grew in size. Joe and Ian grabbed their spears.

"Ryan, it's time for you to go to the door and turn the Key," Joe pleaded.

As the smoke continued to grow, a figure began to form from it.

"It's the Dark Shadow!" yelled Ian. "Everyone move back!"

At that moment, Tarien and James grabbed Haley's arms and moved as far back as possible. They called out to Ryan, who was fixated on the forming body of the Dark Shadow—its red eyes, its black scaly skin, and fire coursing through its veins. He was not going to leave them to fend off the Dark Shadow alone. Ryan moved over and stood side by side with Ian and Joe. With darkness all around it, the Dark Shadow opened its mouth, and a loud shriek rang out; causing the group to cover their ears. With its mouth open, the noise continued as smoke seeped out. Ryan watched as the strings of smoke continued to spew out to the right and left of the Dark Shadow, until they formed five separate figures.

As the Dark Shadow shut its mouth, the noise ceased. Now ahead of them were five mirror images of the Dark Shadow standing beside the original. The similarities between them were uncanny.

"Get ready!" yelled Joe as he handed Ryan a bag of the crystals. "Toss them now," he shouted to Ryan.

As the blue crystals rained in the air, the Dark Shadow and its five clones evaporated, leaving a trail of smoke. Ian, Joe, and Ryan stood motionless, only to see the six figures reemerge in front of them. As they appeared, the blue crystals exploded tossing light in all directions. As the light pierced through them, the clones became visible, creating a momentary puncture through their bodies. Once the light passed, they again became replicas of the Dark Shadow, making it impossible to decipher which was the original.

The six Dark Shadows moved in and out of the air as they attacked Ryan, Joe, and Ian. Twirling their spears with speed and efficiency, Ian and Joe fought off each enemy that lunged toward them. Meanwhile, Ryan held off the onslaught by generating a white force field of light in front of him with his hands; trying to keep the enemy at bay. As he pushed his hands forward, darkness began to seep through. Ian and Joe continued to use their speed to fend off the enemy, but Ryan's strength was beginning to wane. The constant blows from the Dark Shadows pounding on Ryan's energy field became too much. His last-ditch effort to pull in additional energy failed as the power he created broke down and the figures crashed through his body—knocking him down to the ground.

"Wake up, Champ." Ryan opened his eyes at the sound of the voice. Looking around, he noted he was in a room that was all white. He recognized the voice but saw no one.

"Dad, where are you?" he asked. "I can hear you but I can't see you."

He walked around the room looking for an exit—but there were no doors. Beginning to panic, he frantically touched the walls, in hopes of finding a way out. He stopped his movement when he noticed something carved into the wall. He moved closer to see it.

The lettering was miniscule, but as he drew closer, he read it out loud, "Electricity fears no one." Ryan read it over and over again. "What does it mean?" he said as he banged his head against the wall. He continued to bang his head until he felt lightheaded and dizzy. As he attempted to walk, he stumbled down to the floor. As he fell, he muttered out, "Electricity."

Light entered his eyes, and Ryan felt a tingling sensation in his hands. He felt a buildup of power on his fingertips. He began to move the force inside him, up into the palms of his hands. The spears of Joe and Ian could be heard piercing through the Dark Shadows, as Ryan gathered himself and stood up. At this moment, Ryan felt strength he never had before. He raised his hands up toward the Dark Shadows ahead of him, and bolts of electricity came exploding out of his open palms. The figures realizing Ryan was still alive turned their attention away from Ian and Joe and squarely on Ryan.

"Now is the time!" Joe yelled.

With his power creating immense sparks of electricity around him, Ryan pounded his hands together, sending forward massive bolts of blinding light. The Dark Shadows, not prepared for such power, were pierced through—screeching out in pain. The clones began to disintegrate back into black smoke, falling down to the floor. Meanwhile, the original Dark Shadow, now alone, shrieked uncontrollably as it fell apart. As it did, the fire inside its body poured out like lava. The Dark Shadow continued to turn and twist as the liquid fire was flushed out. Its legs disintegrated first, and its body collapsed.

Haley, James, and Tarien ran over to Ryan. "You did it!" Haley said with excitement.

Just as they had started to celebrate, a ball of fire was launched from the disintegrating hand of the Dark Shadow. The fire left its hand with such ferocity that Ian, without enough time to react, was struck through the chest. It crushed through him and knocked him down.

"No! No! It was supposed have been over. We defeated them," Ryan said as he pleaded with Ian to get up. "You can't go, Ian. I have already lost too much."

Ian seemingly in minimal pain, smiled at Ryan and said, "You have not lost anything, son." Ian's body swiftly turned into dust and twisted upward.

CHAPTER 33

The Test

With the disintegration of the Dark Shadow complete and Ian's body now gone, the remaining members of the group gathered around a disheartened Ryan. Haley and Tarien put their hands on his shoulders as Ryan lowered his head to gather himself.

Joe stood in front of him and said, "Now it is time, Ryan. It is time to finish your mission."

Ryan lifted his head toward Joe and knew he was right. He picked himself up, pulled the Key out of his pocket, and looked over at Haley, James, and Tarien.

"Guys, there is really nothing left for you to do. We defeated the Devamans. It is time that you guys finish your journey and enter into the Realm."

The three of them looked at each other, and Haley replied, "We started this journey together, and we will finish together."

James chimed in next. "Turn the Key. We will wait here for you."

Ryan smiled at the three friends he had made during his time in the Blue Alley, motioned to Joe, and said, "Let's go." The two walked toward the marble door. As they neared, the glow returned to the Key once again.

Ryan pulled on the white handle, and the door swung open. A surge of air was released from inside. Holding onto the Key tightly, Ryan walked toward the unknown, his heart thumping loudly out of his chest. As he made his way inside, he turned back to Joe.

"Good luck, Ryan. Always remember who you are. I have to close the door now. It cannot remain open when the Key is turned."

Ryan nodded at Joe and watched as the door closed, wondering if this was the last time he would see Joe. Ryan turned and looked at his surroundings. He saw a staircase several feet ahead of him that led straight up. The light inside the room was dim, but above the staircase, he could see various colored lights nearly thirty feet above him. Ryan walked slowly to the staircase and began to climb up.

Nearly halfway to the top, a thrashing sound was heard coming from below. "Joe, is that you?" he shouted down. When there was no response, he continued moving up. As he neared the top, the lighting became brighter, and the whispering voice reemerged, repeating his name. "Ryan, why are you so afraid to give in to your fears?" the whispering voice said. As Ryan pulled himself up over the top of the staircase, he felt a thunderous pain pounding inside his head. A burst of images flashed before his eyes. One image in particular haunted Ryan: the vision of his father's cold, pale body lying motionless in the casket. Ryan closed his eyes and stumbled down onto one knee. He shook his head, trying to remove the image. Eventually able to pull himself up from the floor, the pain fled from his body.

Ryan standing up and gazing out in front of him realized the lights inside were coming from various crystal windows at the back of the room. Remembering the task at hand, he moved forward. Ahead of him, was a metal bridge twenty-five feet in length. At the end of it were two steps leading to a circular table that was held up by a five-foot marble beam. From a distance, the table appeared to be releasing a blue glow.

Ryan slowly made his way to the bridge. As he walked, he was crushed with a jarring shot of pain in his head. Ryan closed his eyes and the memory of the fight he had with his father the day he passed, played in his mind. The guilt was too much to bear. He watched on as they fought about his grades. Hearing the argument and the immaturity in his reaction to his Father, Ryan yelled, "Dad, I'm right here! I am so sorry. You were right along." Yet his father did not respond, and Ryan soon realized that he could neither be heard nor seen. As the scene continued to unfold, Ryan watched as his father grabbed the car keys to leave. Ryan yelled out to his father, "Dad, please don't go! You cannot get into that car. I am begging you." Ryan's plea went unheard, and tears poured down his face, as he watched his father leave the house.

Ryan opened his eyes, put his hands on his head in despair, and yelled out, "Leave me alone!" Ryan gathered enough strength to continue forward on the metal bridge. He was nearly halfway to the glowing blue table, but the closer he got, the stronger the blasts of pain came crashing at him—one causing him to stumble down to the floor and close his eyes.

Ryan opened his eyes and found himself inside a car. "Hey, Champ."

Ryan was excited at the sound of his father's voice. He was sitting in the passenger seat of his father's car. He stared at his father, ecstatic to see him again. He looked at his father's movements and mannerisms and felt a sense of joy. But it did not last long, as he realized his father had just left the voice message on Ryan's phone before the car accident. A sense of uneasiness gripped Ryan. He moved forward in his seat, trying to get his father's attention, shouting out continuously, "Please stop the car!"

But his father could not hear him. Ryan proceeded to attempt to grab the steering wheel of the car to change its course, but the wheel did not budge. With the car continuing down the highway, Ryan looked around, watching each car that passed, afraid that at any moment, the car would be struck.

"It's not too late, dad. There is still time." As he said this, a twenty-year-old driving a black SUV in the left lane lost control and sideswiped his father's car, causing him to lose his grip of the steering wheel. As the car spun, Ryan's father tried to steady it. Ryan held onto to the side of the car door until the car stopped spinning. Trying to regain his wits, Ryan looked up and a light came racing toward them. The approaching truck attempted to slow down, but it was too late. It slammed head-on into his father's car.

"No! No!" Ryan screamed—his hands on his head and his eyes closed. When he opened his eyes, he found himself back on the bridge. As he tried to pick himself up, he was crushed down to the ground as yet another thunderous image flashed into his head. He was now in front of his father's car, which was completely totaled. He heard the sound of glass breaking under his shoes as he walked. The glass was scattered all over the road. Lights flashed all around him. He looked up and noted two police cars and an ambulance nearing the scene. With the lights creeping closer, Ryan was given enough visibility to see his father's body in the car; covered in blood. Ryan fell to his knees in agony and muttered, "I can't anymore. Just please make it stop." Trying to rid himself of the image, he shut his eyes and let his head sink down.

Feeling a cold surface under his hands, he opened his eyes and found himself on a white tile floor. Confused by his new surroundings, Ryan gazed up and realized he was on the fifth floor of the same hospital where his father had passed. He was in the same exact position he'd been in when he'd collapsed after learning of his father's death. Yet this time, the hospital was not filled with the movement of doctors, nurses, patients, and family members. The lighting in the hospital was bleary, and there were no sounds at all—the hospital was silent and empty. As Ryan sat up, a noise came from the hallway to his left. Ryan could not make out what it was, until the sound drew closer—footsteps.

Ryan tried to stand up, but he was too exhausted from the pain he had endured. The footsteps became louder as they reached the corner right by Ryan. *Who is it?* A pair of black casual work shoes appeared, worn by a man dressed in an elegant black business suit. The gentleman was perfectly groomed, his hair styled with precision, his face clean shaven, and his suit impeccably ironed. Sitting on the hospital floor, Ryan looked up as the man strolled over to him.

"Hi, Ryan," the man calmly said as he put his hands out to help Ryan off the ground. Ryan reached out for the man's hands and was lifted off the floor. Unable to stand on his own, Ryan let the man support him into a nearby chair.

"Thank you so much for your help," Ryan said. "Do we know each other from somewhere?"

The man looked at Ryan with a smile and said, "We have never had the pleasure to meet, but I can tell you, it is an honor to make your acquaintance, Ryan. You are a very popular young man."

Confused, Ryan asked, "Am I dreaming? Where is everybody?"

The man looked at Ryan and replied, "Son, this is not a dream, but a place and time that we were destined to meet at. I did not choose this location; you did. You tell me, then—why are we here?"

Still feeling lethargic, Ryan responded, "This is the hospital where my father was brought after his accident. And this was about the spot where the doctors came and told me and my family that there was nothing else they could do for him."

The man, showing true concern for Ryan, put his hand on Ryan's shoulder and said, "I am so sorry for your loss and all of the pain you have been carrying. One should not be expected to carry such a burdensome weight in life. It does not feel right for someone so good to be handed such a bad card. It then, begs the question: why do bad things happen to good people?"

Ryan looked at the man and shook his head in agreement.

"Did your father deserve to die, while the thieves, murderers, rapists, and other criminals in the world get to continue living their lives? Why do kids die? Why does a mother get in a car accident because of a drunk driver while criminals live well into their nineties? Does this sound fair to you, Ryan?" the man asked with passion in his voice.

The man stood up and continued to preach to Ryan. "This is not the way I believe life should be. It should not be filled with so much sorrow, anger, hate, and pain. You, Ryan, should not have to deal with this at such a young age. How do you feel, Ryan?"

Ryan looked up at the man and said, "I feel tired and crushed inside."

"Of course you do!" the man replied. "It's the unfairness of life. You know what? Let me help you with that burden. I can alleviate some of that pain."

Ryan's curiosity was enticed. He looked up at the man and asked, "How can you possibly do that?"

The man looked at Ryan with a concerned face and said, "You are holding onto an item that is compounding all the pain inside of you and not allowing you to be free from life's struggles. Let me take it so that you can finally be free."

As the man finished speaking, Ryan asked, "What item are you speaking of?"

The man pointed at Ryan's jeans and said, "It is inside your pocket, and all you have to do is hand it over to me."

Ryan pondered the pain and suffering he had endured over the past months and how badly he wanted to be liberated from it. He put his hand in his right pocket and put his fingers on the Key. "Are you sure about this? I think I'm supposed to be doing something with it."

Slightly more assertive, the man countered, "You are supposed to hand it over so that someone else can carry the weight for you."

Trying to process the situation, Ryan pulled the Key out of his pocket and held it in his right hand. "I am just so drained," Ryan whispered as he reached out to hand the Key over to the man, but before the man could grab the Key from him, a voice was heard echoing through the hospital—repeating one word: "Champ."

"Hand over the Key, Ryan. You will never be free," the man pleaded as Ryan put the Key back in his pocket and moved toward the voice. As Ryan walked, he noticed that the voice was coming from the hospital room where his father had passed away.

"Champ," the voice whispered again.

"Ryan, there is nothing there for you but more heartache," the man shouted as Ryan had begun to enter the room.

Ryan stepped in, and held onto the wall as a crutch. The torture he endured had taken a toll on him. He looked around the room, but no one was inside. The room was perfectly clean. The bed was made, and nothing was out of place. Ryan hung his head in disappointment at the lack answers inside the room.

"Ryan, come back outside!" the man shouted from the hallway. With nothing inside the room for Ryan, he started to walk out when, out of the corner of his eye, he noticed an object on the floor by the bed. He cautiously went over and leaned down to pick it up. He grabbed the object, opened up his hand—it was a brown leather wristband he had never seen before. The front side of the wristband did contain any verbiage, yet when he turned it over, engraved into the leather was the word *Champ.* As Ryan read the word out loud, he remembered his mission.

Taking the wristband with him, Ryan walked out of the room and into the hallway. The man was standing with his back toward him. "I think I will hold onto the Key for a little while longer," Ryan said to the man.

As the words came out of Ryan's mouth, the man did not flinch or acknowledge Ryan. "Did you hear me? You can leave now. I don't need your help!" Ryan shouted.

The man lowered his head, and as he did, black smoke began to hover around him. Within a second, the man surged at Ryan and was standing face to face with him, his eyes as red as fire. The man whispered, "Darkness will never leave. You cannot escape it." And with that, the man vanished into thin air with a thunderous blast, knocking Ryan down to the floor.

Ryan's eyes opened, and he felt the bridge underneath him. He was once again inside the room by the Realm. As he looked around, thick black smoke was gathered around him. Now more determined than ever to finish the job and unwilling to let the enemy defeat him, Ryan picked himself up and pushed through the smoke.

As he trudged forward he heard whispering voices telling him to give up. But Ryan continued and used his hands to wave off the smoke, as he followed the glow of the table ahead. Steps away from the table, the voices whispered, "You will never be rid of us, Ryan." Ryan ignored the voices and was now in front of the two small steps that led to the table. The whispering voices unrelenting, tried to corrupt his mind with thoughts of evil. At that moment, Ryan reached into his pocket, pulled out the Key and walked up the two steps. He looked down into the table in front of him. As he gazed upon the table, there was a ring of crystals circling around a keyhole, creating a blue radiance. With the Key in his right hand, Ryan lifted it, slipped the key into the hole, and closed his eyes, blocking out all of the noise. A vision came to him. It was of him and his father playing baseball in the backyard. As the vision passed, he opened his eyes and, turned the Key.

The blue glow from the crystals raced out of the table and shot up into the air, covering the entire room. With an eruption of speed, the blue light raced across the room, expelling all of the smoke inside. The light continued down the staircase and vanished. He looked down at the table and the crystals were now white. He looked out of the windows in the room and saw a shockwave of blue light traveling across the beach and moving throughout the rest of the Blue Alley. His mission now complete, Ryan turned to walk back toward the marble door when he felt something missing—the Key. He looked back at the table. It was gone, as was the keyhole it was placed in.

CHAPTER 34

The Realm

As he went down the staircase and reached the entrance, he paused for a moment and opened the door. The air and the light from outside surged into the room, and Ryan felt tranquility. He stepped out into the Third Post and the first one to greet him was Haley. Her beautiful face had a smile as she lunged toward Ryan to hug him.

"You did it," she whispered into his ear and they held each other tightly.

"Let us have a chance at him," Tarien said as he and James came over to shake hands and congratulate Ryan. And then there was Joe. He walked over to Ryan with his usual stoic composure and said, "Never had a doubt, kid. Never! We are now safe because of you." He cracked a smile and embraced him with a hug, and whispered, "I am so proud of you."

"Okay, I think it's finally time we enter the Realm," James ecstatically proclaimed.

The group walked toward the entrance of the Realm; reveling in its beauty. As they walked, Ryan reached out to hold Haley's hand, and she held on tight.

"I thought you were going to just make sure that I made it to the Realm and then head back," Haley said to Ryan with a smile.

"Maybe I will stick around for a little bit," Ryan replied.

"What changed your mind?" she asked him.

Grinning, he said, "Someone I recently met."

They laughed out loud as they neared the opening of the Realm.

The entrance to the Realm was made up of a sizable, round cylinder door connected to the massive marble walls. The door was made of frosted glass—not allowing one to see inside. In the middle of the entrance door, in blue lettering was the word "*Pacem.*" When they reached the front entrance, they paused.

Tarien said, "Joe, what do we do now? How do we get inside?"

The building began to divide in two, causing the group to take a couple steps back. As they stared, the glass of the building parted, and out came the brightest light one could ever imagine. Ryan put his hands up to block the light, but he soon realized that although the light was projecting all around him, it neither affected his vision nor wounded his eyes. The light brought serenity and warmth. After a few seconds, the glass entrance doors opened completely and the light slowly faded. Standing in front of the group were two guards dressed in matching brown military style uniforms, each standing firmly upright and holding a spear. Joe approached the guard who was standing to their left and whispered into his ear. As he finished, the guard nodded and went back to his position.

Joe moved back to the group.

"Joe what did you tell him?" Ryan asked. "And what are we supposed to do now?"

Joe looked at them and said, "It's time to go inside." With these words, their faces lit up. The first to make a move toward the guards were Tarien and James. As they neared, the guards blocked the entrance with their spears, startling the two. The guards stared at them intensely. Moments later, they lifted theirs spears and opened the path for Tarien and James to enter. "See you guys in the Realm!" James said with a childlike smile on his face. They slowly walked past the guards, entered the building with their bags and went into a circular room filled with light seeping in from all angles through the crystal glass. Ahead of them, there did not seem to be an exit. When they reached the middle of the room, the glass on the other side began to slide open. Light beamed through the glass doors as they opened, but once more, it had a welcoming feel. Seconds later, the light faded, and ahead of them was beautiful brick pathway whose end could not be seen. As Tarien and James walked toward the pathway, Tarien looked back at his friends and yelled, "See you on the other side!" Tarien and James walked past the glass doors, onto the pathway, and out of sight.

Amazed and anxious, Haley and Ryan were ready to continue the journey. They slowly strolled over toward the guards, holding hands, nervous of the unknown journey they were about to embark on. They continued forward until the guards once again blocked the entrance with their spears. Filled with excitement at the idea of entering the Realm, they looked at each other and smiled. The wait to get inside took longer than that of Tarien and James as the guards continued to block the entrance. Ryan looked back at Joe, who was several feet behind them. For the first time, Joe looked nervous. Ryan let go of Haley's hand and turned his head. "Joe, what is wrong? What is going on that you're not telling me?"

As he stared at Joe, he heard Haley say, "Ryan, they are letting us in. We can go."

Ryan turned back to the guards, who were no longer blocking the entrance. They walked side by side, about to pass the guards, when the guard to their left blocked Ryan's path, while the other guard kept his spear up, allowing Haley to continue. "What is going on here?" Ryan yelled out. "Move out of my way and let me in," he shouted at the guard. He looked at Haley and back at Joe. "Joe, tell them to let me through," Ryan said.

"I can't do that, Ryan. They will not let you in."

Anger boiled inside of him, and Ryan snapped, "What do you mean? Why wouldn't they let me in?"

Joe moved closer to Ryan and said, "Because you're not meant to go in."

Ryan let the words sink in for a second and then lunged forward, trying to pass the guards. As he did, the guard to his left forcefully pushed Ryan back. He continued to fight, unwilling to give up. It was useless, as the strength of the guard was to powerful, and Ryan tumbled to the ground. As he fell, the guard immediately went back to his post, joining the other.

With tears rolling down her face, Haley went over to help Ryan up from the ground.

"This is all your doing, Joe! Isn't it? You whispered something to him!" Ryan yelled angrily as he stood back up. "You tell me I'm so important, you ask me to complete this mission—only to tell me I am not welcome. Why?"

Joe walked over to Haley and told her, "Go inside, Haley. You will find all the answers you are searching for."

Tears flowing profusely down her cheeks, Haley replied, "I am not going to leave Ryan."

Joe whispered to Haley as he gently grabbed her hand, "You are not leaving him. You will see each other again. Your mother is inside waiting for you, and so is the rest of your life. Ryan will follow, but before he does, I need to talk to him."

"You promise I will see him again?"

Joe, still holding her hand, replied, "I promise."

Completely shaken by the recent events, Ryan looked at Haley and said, "Go inside and find your mother. I will meet up with you soon. You need to find out where Dylan is."

Once he finished speaking Haley lunged toward Ryan and gave him a kiss on his lips. Initially caught by surprise, Ryan quickly reciprocated the kiss. They embraced each other for a few seconds, but for the two of them, it was worth every moment. As they let each other go, Ryan grabbed Haley's hand. When their fingers slipped away from each other, Ryan said, "I will see you soon."

Still in tears, Haley walked toward the guards. This time they stood straight, and did not block her path. She passed the guards, stepped inside, and walked a couple of feet. She stood still for a few seconds and, turned to Ryan—tears no longer visible—and said, "Everything is going to be all right." She turned back and walked toward the pathway. Ryan, unwilling to let her go, made one last attempt to get inside, but before he could leap toward the guards, Joe grabbed him by the arm, causing him to lose his footing. As he tumbled down, he looked out to find Haley, but instead saw a girl who was no more than eight or nine years of age walking onto the pathway and out of sight.

As he hit the ground, Ryan quickly stood up and yelled out to Joe, "What happened to Haley? All I saw was a little girl with Haley's bag who wasn't her. Just let me inside to make sure she is all right." As he pointed to the entrance, a figure appeared from the pathway, making its way to the circular room.

"Calm down, Ryan," Joe said. "It will all be explained."

"How can you tell me to calm down? This whole journey has been filled with so many mysteries, and just when I thought I had it figured out, something new happens. I am just so tired!" Ryan proclaimed, holding back tears and placing his hands over his head. All he could think of, was Haley was gone.

CHAPTER 35

Journey's End

"Is everything okay?" a man asked from behind Ryan.

Taking his hands off his head, Ryan turned around. The voice came from a young man, maybe only four years older than Ryan. The man was dressed in khakis and a green collared shirt, and was of average height and build.

Still upset, Ryan blurted out, "Who are you and what do you want?"

The man looked at Ryan, smiled, and walked over to Joe. The two embraced and shared pleasantries as the young man congratulated Joe on making it to the Realm. "I knew you would do it. I knew you would safely guide him," the man said. The two shook hands and spoke of seeing each other inside the Realm.

Ryan confused, and visibly upset, said to the man, "Excuse me, but maybe you can help me out here."

The man looked at Ryan once again and smiled. "How can I help you, Ryan?"

Eager to explain the situation, he said, "For some reason, these guards of yours won't let me in."

The man listened to what Ryan had to say and turned around. To Ryan's surprise, the man walked over to the guards and whispered to them. He came back to Ryan and said, "Follow me."

Before they went any further, Joe spoke, "Well, I think my job here is done." He walked over to the young man and once again shook his hand. Joe fighting back his emotions turned to Ryan, "I am so proud of you, and I am so happy that I got the chance to take this journey with you. There was not a second that I didn't think you would succeed. You are natural leader with a solid heart. Don't lose any of that, kid."

Realizing his time with Joe was coming to an end, Ryan responded, "Joe, I'm sorry for giving you a hard time." Joe placed his hand on Ryan's shoulder and told him not to worry. "You protected me, and you watched over me. I don't know I how I can ever repay you," Ryan said as he shook Joe's hand.

"It was my honor," Joe said. The two hugged, and as they did, Joe whispered, "I hope you get your answers!" They let go of each other, and Joe walked toward the guards and into the circular room. He turned back and smiled at Ryan before going down the path and vanishing from sight.

With Joe now gone, the young man turned to Ryan and said, "You ready?" Ryan nodded and followed the man. As he stood in front of the guards with the man by his side, they put their spears down, preventing them from walking in. Ryan looked at the man, but within seconds, the guards lifted their spears and opened the way for Ryan to enter. Ryan could not move. The young man gave Ryan a pat on the back encouraging him to enter. Finally able get his feet moving, he stepped forward, passed the guards and entered the circular room. The room was filled with positive energy. The lights from outside gushed through the crystal glass windows. All of the symbols and scribes he had seen along the journey were carved into the surrounding glass.

"Thank you for getting me inside. I am not sure what the issue was before."

As Ryan looked upon the symbols, the man spoke up. "Hey, Champ."

The words and the voice—Ryan knew them both so well. He shut his eyes, and hoped his mind was not playing a trick on him. He turned around with his eyes still closed. Ryan opened his eyes gently. When they opened, Ryan's legs became weak and his heart began to race. "Dad?" Ryan said as the man he had prayed to see for the past several months was now in front of him. Unsure if it was a deception created by the Devamans, Ryan was hesitant to believe.

"Champ, it's me," said the young man.

Still uneasy, Ryan asked "If you are my father, then tell me something only he would know. What happened the night we played Benferd High?

The young man smiled and said, "Thought you were going to give me a hard one. That night you hit two homeruns and would have won the game if it were not for that umpire calling our guy out in the last inning. And you remember what happened after that play?"

Ryan stared at the man for a moment, and then, with huge smile on his face, he said, "You were thrown out of the game for arguing with the umpire." As he said this, he ran into his father's arms and whispered, "I missed you so much!

"Am I dreaming all of this?" Ryan continued as he embraced his father.

Holding on tight to his son, his father replied, "This is all real, Champ. Everything here is real."

When Ryan finally let go of his father, he looked up at him, tears streaming down his face and said, "How is this possible?"

His father looked at Ryan and replied, "How I missed you, my son. I knew you would find your way to me."

Ryan began to speak rapidly, as his emotions raced. "Dad, I have been so torn up and sad without you. There is a hole in me that I can't seem to fill. When I wake up every day, I feel as if something is off in my life. Regret eats at me. I wish I had helped you out more when you asked me to do things around the house. I wish I had spent more time with you like you wanted. How do I fix my regrets?"

When he finished speaking, he was out of breath. Ryan's father put his hand on his shoulder and said, "Son, look at me." Ryan lifted his head up to look at his father. "Don't be sad. Life is a just like a book. My story was filled with so much happiness and love. All of my chapters and pages were filled with everything I wanted in life. But my story came to an end. Now it is time for you to write your book and your pages with memories of joy, laughter, and happiness. Drop your regrets, because you were everything I wanted in a son. All books run out of pages. Some will end early and others later, but how you fill your pages with the time you're given is what truly matters. I am so happy that I got all my memories with you. I am so thankful I got to see you grow up, see you play baseball, see you become a man, and see you be happy. I'm at peace now, Champ. It's time to put your tears for me away."

With tears rolling down, Ryan said, "Dad, I get angry every time I think of how you were taken away from me. I need you back to help guide me. I don't want my memories of you to fade with time."

Ryan's father reached out and grabbed his son's hand. "Our memories will never fade, my son. We will always be connected."

As Ryan looked at his father, he said, "I don't know who I am anymore. I have lost my direction."

Giving his son a hug, Ryan's father said, "I know exactly the man I helped raise. That's someone with a good heart and a gentle soul who is kind and loving. Someone with faith who will do what is right and will be a leader. I couldn't be more proud. It's time, Champ; you show the rest of the world what I have always seen in you. Do you think they would have chosen someone who doesn't have all these attributes to protect this place? Let go of the anger, son."

Pointing to two small benches in the room to their left, his father said, "Let's sit down to talk. There is much to discuss."

CHAPTER 36

Where Am I?

At this point, Ryan's eyes were red from all the tears he had shed. As they sat down, Ryan began to ask all the questions he could think of. "Where are we? Is this heaven?"

With a grin on his face, his father replied, "This place goes by many different names. I am sure you have heard it called the Realm. But the name is irrelevant, because to each person, it means something different. It's a place of peace."

Ryan quickly fired another question. "Are my grandparents, aunt, and uncles here too?"

His dad looked at Ryan and replied, "Yes, they are, and they always keep a close eye on you, more than you know."

"I lost so many people on my way over. What happens to them?"

"They are just fine, son. They are better off than before—full of peace. I wish I could have been out there with you but it was too early for me."

"Were you the young man I saw outside? I haven't seen him since."

Smiling, his dad responded, "This place provides everyone with the unique ability to present themselves in different lights. Who you saw outside of the Realm was me, but it was the version of me at twenty-four years of age. That was the age I was when your mother and I got married. That moment is so special to me, because not only did I marry the woman of my dreams, it was the start of our family, which led to us having a son. See, someone outside of the Realm or looking from the outside in will see the representation of a time that each person holds most dear to them. That is why you saw me that way—because that is the moment in time that I chose to portray. Once you enter the Realm, you will see someone the way you want to remember them, and that is why you now see me."

Trying to take all of this in, Ryan said, "Is that why I saw Haley's image change?"

His father replied, "Yes, her image changed to a time when she was truly happy in her life."

Still not comprehending what his father was saying, Ryan asked, "So what if someone passes away as a baby or a young child? What would they look like?"

His father grinned at his question and said, "You always were thinker, Champ. In those occasions, they would choose to portray themselves to everyone as who they would have been at a certain time in their lives."

Ryan stood up. "Dad, why can't I stay here with you? I can't lose you again. Also, Haley and I—"

His father stood up before Ryan could finish. "Ryan, your job here is done. It's time for you to go home—time for you to be with your mother, your family, and your friends. Haley opened your heart and showed how powerful love can be. She showed you that life is not worth living if you don't have someone by your side to share it. You will find this love, but for now, you need to be free of the anger inside."

Shaking his head in disagreement, Ryan said, "I don't know how to live without you."

Ryan's father put his hand on Ryan's shoulder and said, "Champ, I will always be by your side in everything you do. I will be there in your next baseball game, I will be there when you go to college, when you get married, and when you start your own family. Be bold in life and enjoy the journey. I will always be there."

Ryan sat down on the bench. Tears welled up in his eyes.

"Son, don't cry. I am so happy here. I am here with your grandparents and the rest of our family and friends who have passed on. One day, Ryan, we will see each other again. And on that day, you and I will throw the baseball around and play catch. But right now, it's time for you to move on. You will always have our memories and everything I taught you. Carry them in your heart and let them guide you."

Ryan looked up at his father, stood up, and held onto him for dear life. "I will never forget," he whispered. "You are my hero, dad. I love you so much."

As they held onto each other, his dad whispered, "I love you, Champ. I will always be there with you."

His father's voice began to fade as Ryan felt a strong tug on his back and he began to fall backward. As he fell, his father's image became less visible. Before the image left, he yelled out, "Dad, I love you!"

CHAPTER 37

Free Fall

As he continued his free fall down, the light from the room converged on Ryan. It blocked his view of his father, of the room, and of the Realm. Images began to display in front of him. The first image was of his first cousin Carol, who was crying as she lay in a hospital bed, holding infant triplets who had passed away while she gave birth. As the image faded, another appeared. It was his mother, showing an eight-year-old Ryan a picture of him hugging a dog that passed when Ryan was three. The light once again took over Ryan's view until a new vision appeared in front of him, this time of when he was ten years of age and sitting down with his father in his office as they looked at history books. His father would show him pictures of his uncle—his mother's brother—who was a military soldier. In one mission his uncle saved his entire squad from an ambush by enemy forces. As he got the final squad member out safely, he was shot in the back. The image moved away, and Ryan continued his free fall, the light still swarming around him. The next image was of him and his grandparents from his father's side, sitting on the couch and yelling at the television screen while watching Jeopardy. A five-year-old Ryan laughed as his grandmother and grandfather yelled out the answers and competed against each other. The image faded away, and another followed. He saw himself sitting on his mother's lap as she showed him pictures of her family. A six-year-old Ryan kept laughing at one picture of his mom at the beach with his grandfather, her father, as she was burying him in sand.

As this image floated away, Ryan could hear a beeping noise in the distance. The noise increased in volume as he continued his descent, piecing his journey together and realizing he was never alone.

His descent slowed, and suddenly the noise and the light vanished. Silence was all around. Ryan's body collided with an object, and all went dark.

Still in the dark, Ryan heard the noise again. He could not figure out where it was coming from. A beeping noise continued as Ryan fought to open his eyelids. He felt a throbbing pain on the right side of his head. Frustrated, he took a deep breath, and as he did, he heard his father's voice. "Always and forever, Champ." At that moment Ryan used all his strength and gradually opened his eyes. He was lying in a hospital bed. In discomfort, he raised his hand and felt bandages heavily wrapped around the top of his forehead. He gazed around the room and saw flowers, balloons and get well wishes. Exhaustion crept in. Ryan closed his eyes and slept.

CHAPTER 38

Champ Forever

"Wait, so this whole thing was a dream? He was in the hospital the entire time?" Michael asked his father.

"Why do you say that, son?" his father asked.

With a face full of disappointment, Michael replied, "Because obviously he could not have found the Key, the Blue Alley, and the Realm while lying in a hospital bed. Ugh!"

The father laughed and gave Michael a hug. As he did, a woman's voice called from the bedroom door, "Okay, you two, it's time for bed."

"Mom, did you know the story dad just told me?"

The woman smiled and replied, "Is your father trying to sell you the Realm story?"

She walked into the room, and her pregnant figure became visible. She gave Michael a kiss, wished him a good night, and looked over at her husband as they walked together towards the door, "I can't believe you told him that story."

"Dad, so it wasn't a real?"

"Son, does it matter if it's real or not? What matters is that you understand the meaning behind it."

Putting his head down on his pillow, Michael replied, "I think I get it. My family will always be beside me, and no matter what, you will always be there for me."

Before turning the light off in the room, his father gave Michael a wink and said, "Good night, son."

Michael's father entered an office inside the house and turned on the light. In the middle of the room was a mahogany desk, and two mahogany bookshelves against the wall. Various pictures were displayed on the wall and bookshelves. He walked over to the desk, pulled out a brown leather chair, and sat down. He opened the bottom right drawer of the desk. He pulled out a manila folder, placed it down on the desk, and opened it up. Inside was a notepad that was headlined "A Son's Journey." Beneath the headline was a multitude of paragraphs. As he flipped through the sheets, he reached the moment where he had last written and began to fill the pages.

Once he finished writing, he placed the folder back into the drawer and looked around the room. The story of his life played out in the pictures and accolades all around. He looked at the frames on the desk. There was a picture of him, his wife, and Michael at the park. Next to this was his wedding picture, followed by a picture of him and Michael at a football game. He gazed at the items on the wall, which included his college degree, pictures of him playing baseball in college, and trophies on a bookshelf. He paused and stared at a framed picture of him and his father. The picture was of them smiling as they sat in the stands at a baseball game. As he stared at the picture and thought of his life, a smile came to his face, and he whispered, "Always and forever."

The End

KGML

Printed in the United States
By Bookmasters